DEADLY

Intersections

Ann Roberts

Bella
BOOKS

2011

Acknowledgments

I've loved mysteries since I was a kid. The first mystery I remember was the original *Scooby Doo*, a real whodunit with a plot, suspects and a villain. I loved watching Velma, the smart girl, and Daphne, the pretty girl, and I thought it would be cool to have a big dog. Then there was Nancy Drew, Encyclopedia Brown and Ellery Queen. Over a bowl of popcorn I watched all the crime shows and movies with my dad, and during commercials we discussed all the suspects and motives. If you're reading this series, you love mysteries too, and I'm eternally grateful for your support. And I thank Anna Chinappi, my editor, for tightening the dialogue, and as always, I'm grateful to Bella Books for continuing to publish my stories. Finally, without the support of my family, including three very large dogs, I wouldn't find the time to write.

About the Author

Ann Roberts is the author of *Paid in Full*, *Furthest from the Gate*, *Brilliant*, *Beach Town*, *White Offerings*, *Root of Passion*, *Beacon of Love*, and *Keeping up Appearances*.

A native Arizonan who should've been born near an ocean and a lighthouse, Ann and her family go to a coast as often as possible. She and her partner recently celebrated their sixteenth anniversary, and she wonders how such a wonderful woman would tolerate living with a writer for so long.

CHAPTER ONE

Usually people she'd just met weren't found dead two hours later, but trouble always seemed to follow Ari Adams. The victim had seemed much taller than he did now, crumpled over the steering wheel, the horn blaring inside the parking garage.

No one had given it a thought when it first sounded since it was so common to hear auto alarms randomly trigger in downtown Phoenix. The guests at the annual Phoenix Chamber of Commerce business luncheon continued to enjoy the beautiful February weather on the lawn of Heritage Square, a Phoenix landmark that brought together several old houses onto one property.

Everyone worked the crowd, including Ari and her boss Lorraine Gonzalez. And Ari had learned that commercial real estate was far more lucrative than the residential home market she'd exclusively handled during her twelve-year career as an agent. If they could find one client they'd be set for a few months.

The screeching horn only forced people to lean closer as they spoke to each other but nothing else. Heads finally turned when a woman ran screaming from the garage, her purse swinging from her arm. "Help me! He's dead!"

An older gentleman caught her and held her still while she continued to babble. Ari, a former cop trained to run toward danger and not from it, instantly headed into the garage. She was joined by a few curious businessmen and a security officer who looked as scared as the hysterical woman.

They followed her as she wound her way around the aisles of the garage trying to locate the wailing horn. The ground rumbled as three school buses snaked through the tiny rows toward the exit, their huge engines momentarily interrupting their search. *Probably visiting the Science Center.* Heritage Square bordered the Arizona Science Center, the past and present colliding in the same city block.

She found the car—a Lexus—in the last row, two spaces down from a Mercedes she imagined belonged to the screaming woman who'd left her door wide open. When she looked in the driver's side window, Ari immediately recognized Warren Edgington, an investor and the keynote speaker at the luncheon. She and Lorraine had chatted with him during the meet-and-greet portion. They'd made a connection and he'd taken their cards, mentioning a potential deal they could work together.

"Do any of you guys have a handkerchief?" Ari asked loudly, turning to the three young men who'd followed her.

"Of course," an Adonis-like beefcake said, smiling and offering the white linen square from his breast pocket while the other two stepped away defeated.

She nodded, not returning the smile.

Wrapping her hand around the handkerchief, she pulled at the door handle but it wouldn't open.

"Locked?" Adonis asked.

She nodded and circled the car. She peered inside the passenger's window and noticed an open briefcase with a silver

flask lying inside. A piece of paper rested underneath the flask—
a note.

"This looks like a suicide," Adonis said. He'd moved next to her, so close she could smell his Altoid.

"Maybe," she said as the black and whites pulled up behind the Lexus.

"Now that the cavalry's arrived can I walk you back?" Adonis asked, clearly hopeful.

She offered a little smile, cobbling together a gentle letdown in her mind. She was saved when Colin McDermott, one of her dad's old cronies, stepped from the first car.

"Ari Adams, what in the blazes are you doin' here?"

She met his hug as an answer and noticed Adonis slunk over to a concrete wall.

"I hear your dad's coming to town soon. I can't wait to see him. It's been ages."

She forced a smile. Everyone loved Captain Big Jack Adams, a retired member of the Phoenix Police Department and they looked forward to his arrival—everyone but her. Thinking about his visit the next week gave her heartburn and sent her into a foul mood. She couldn't understand why she'd ever agreed to a reunion. It was too soon and she wasn't ready.

More police officers assembled and a tall blond emerged from an unmarked Caprice. Ari glanced at Adonis, still leaning against the wall. Like her, he was captivated by the statuesque woman with short curly hair who instantly took charge. Ari watched in admiration as she listened to McDermott give her the details. She nodded and scanned the crime scene, her eyes finding Ari. She frowned and came over immediately.

"What are you doing here?"

"Honey, I told you I had a luncheon today, remember?"

Detective Molly Nelson rolled her eyes. "How is it that you're always in the middle of my crime scenes?"

Ari raised a finger to correct her. "That's only happened one other time and look what we got out of it." She offered a slow smile and batted her eyelashes. "Besides I thought you liked it when I surprised you during the workday."

Molly sighed. "I like it *most* of the time. What happened?"

Ari recounted the last ten minutes, assuring Molly she hadn't disturbed the crime scene. "I'd had a very nice chat with him earlier. We kept running into each other, too," she realized.

"What do you mean?"

"Well, he was right behind me in the buffet line, and I saw him again when I went to the ladies room."

Molly raised an eyebrow. "He didn't try to follow you in there, did he?"

"No, it wasn't anything like that. I saw him before I went inside, and when I came out he was arguing with this other guy who'd tried to pick me up earlier after he introduced himself to Lorraine and me."

Molly flipped the page on her notebook. Ari could tell she was in full cop mode because her usual jealous streak didn't surface. "What's his name?"

"The Hometown Grocery Guy, Stan Wertz? We've seen his commercials."

She grimaced. "*He* hit on you? His ads are the worst. So what were they arguing about?"

Ari tried to remember, but she'd been distracted by some drunk women coming out of the powder room. Edgington was standing on the heels of his shoes, arms crossed and shaking his head. Wertz was clearly in his personal space, gesturing with one hand and squeezing Edgington's shoulder with the other. The pose suggested friendly coercion, but Edgington seemed to want no part of it. They were working hard to keep their voices quiet—only the end of sentences grew louder. And she really hadn't been paying close attention.

"I'm not sure. It was definitely about business. Wertz was trying to convince him of something, telling him that it would work, and Edgington kept saying no."

"Did they see you?"

"No, they were really into it when I passed by."

Molly tapped her notebook and gazed at her partner Andre Watson as he watched a lab tech work on Edgington's car. When the door finally opened, the alarm sounded, joining the blaring car horn in a deafening screech until the medical examiner allowed the repositioning of Edgington's body off the steering wheel. When it was finally quiet again, Molly and Ari joined Andre.

"Hey, Ari," Andre said with a smile.

A different tech motioned for Molly, and Ari saw they'd retrieved the flask and the briefcase from the passenger's side. The tech held out the note. *I'm finished. There's no other way,* was written haphazardly in black ink on a sheet of Edgington's personal stationery. Ari noticed a black ink pen rested in the bottom corner of the briefcase.

"Looks like he scribbled this pretty fast," Andre observed.

"We'll have to see if we can have it analyzed," Molly added, "but I'm not too hopeful. If he'd been drinking heavily his penmanship would've been greatly impaired. It'll be difficult to get a match."

"Do you see any more pieces of blank stationery in the briefcase?" Ari asked. "A lot of people don't carry their personal stuff during a workday unless it has a purpose."

Andre checked and found three more sheets, killing Ari's theory that Edgington had definitely planned to kill himself.

Molly stared at Ari. "You were one of the last people to see him alive. Did he seem suicidal to you?"

Ari shrugged. She'd been close to suicide herself but had fooled everyone and nearly died.

Molly's face turned red when she realized what she was asking. "Stupid question. I'm sorry."

"It's okay. And no, I don't think he was suicidal. He hit on me and wanted a date. That's not something you usually do before you commit suicide."

"True," Molly conceded.

She glanced inside. The medical examiner had removed the body and she carefully checked the upholstery with her flashlight. "I don't see any blood, and there's no sign of a struggle."

"I'll run his cell phone records," Andre said. "Maybe he made a call before he offed himself."

"*If* he did it himself," Molly corrected.

"Do you need me for anything else?" Ari asked, looking at her watch.

Molly shook her head. "Not right now."

Ari glanced at Adonis, who was watching them intently. "Honey, I know you're busy, but I need a favor."

"What?" Molly asked, exasperated.

"That guy standing over there is either going to follow me out of this garage and hit on me or he's going to stay and hit on you."

Molly frowned and her eyes found Adonis. Ari knew she hated it when men came on to her. She thought everyone recognized she was a dyke the minute they met her. She didn't understand how beautiful she was to men and women.

"I don't have time for any bullshit today," she murmured, pulling Ari against her for a soft kiss. "Clear enough?" she asked, her voice a ragged whisper.

Ari's throat went dry. Molly had that effect on her. "Quite."

They looked toward Adonis who supported himself against the wall. His jaw dropped.

Two hours later they'd cleared the crime scene. Molly turned toward the skyscraper next to the garage and pointed. "Let's go have a chat with Mr. Wertz and see if he has an alibi for this afternoon."

They found his office high in the sky and she was automatically suspicious. She had a dislike for the rich and powerful that stemmed from her days on the Spokane police force. A rich white boy had been the cause of her former partner's death, at least that's how she'd decided to remember it. *It's the sense of entitlement and the general attitude that they're better than the rest of us. That's what bothers me.*

A receptionist directed them to an inner lobby and Mr. Wertz's personal assistant, Candy. Molly's gaydar activated instantly when Candy's eyes probed *her* body while she ignored Andre, a man who'd been compared to Denzel Washington. Molly doubted he noticed since his gaze never left her voluptuous bosom that was trapped in a too-small silk blouse.

"May I help you?"

She flashed her badge and said, "We need a few minutes with

Mr. Wertz about an incident that happened today at Heritage Square."

"Oh? And if I may ask, how does this involve him?"

She's good, not a pushover. Her job was to keep people *out* of his office, and she scrutinized every request.

"He was there," Andre said curtly. "At the luncheon."

Candy's gaze flicked between them, and Molly noticed the slightest shift in her stony expression. "So you're here about Warren," she stated. She nodded and pressed a series of buttons on the massive communication system in front of her.

"Mr. Wertz? Some detectives need to speak with you about Mr. Edgington."

Interesting. He's Warren to her and Mr. Edgington to Wertz.

She listened to his reply and said, "I'll send them right in."

She escorted them into an immense office, and he stood up, offering a perfect smile with his blindingly glistening teeth. When he extended his hand, she noticed the gold and diamond cufflinks at his wrists that matched the band of his Rolex watch.

"Detectives, how can I help you?"

He motioned for them to sit and returned to the imposing chair behind his massive desk. When he leaned back and crossed his legs, Molly realized he wasn't unusually nervous. *He has nothing to hide or he's a great actor.*

"Mr. Wertz, we're not sure if you've heard. Warren Edgington is dead. He died after the luncheon at Heritage Square."

He nodded. Obviously the news had climbed the twenty-four floors to his office or he had first-hand knowledge, which was why Molly withheld several pieces of key information.

"It's terrible," he said. "Warren and I were business acquaintances. We hadn't worked together, at least not yet. We were pondering a venture, but we hadn't made any definite plans."

"What kind of venture?" Andre asked.

"A land purchase. Warren had a few parcels that I thought might be appropriate for a future Hometown Grocery."

She waited for the usual grief comments that were typical of these interviews, but he offered nothing except facts.

"We understand you were one of the last people to see him alive at the luncheon."

He shifted in his seat. "Yes, we spoke. As a matter of fact we had a few harsh words as well about the land deal. By the end of the conversation I wasn't sure if we could collaborate."

"How did you end the conversation?" Andre asked.

"We didn't, really. It got heated so I walked away, intending to call him later." He chuckled slightly. "I didn't think it was appropriate to argue outside the restrooms."

When Molly looked up from her notes, he was waiting for the next question, his gaze moving between her and Andre.

"Is there anything else?" he asked, trying hard to disguise the impatience in his voice.

"When did you leave the luncheon?" she asked.

"Right after that exchange. The luncheon was over, and people were networking, typical of these events," he said with a wave. "I was frustrated and returned to my office. I believe it was about one o'clock."

"Is there anyone who can verify your return?"

He didn't answer right away as Molly met his stare. He cleared his throat and said, "Fortunately Candy was here so she can vouch for my whereabouts, but most everyone else on this floor takes lunch from twelve-thirty to one-thirty. Any other questions?" he asked emphatically.

"No," she said, rising from the chair.

He escorted them out with a nod of his head and they set their sights on Candy whose fingers flew across her keyboard. When they stopped in front of her desk, she quickly swiveled in her chair to address them. *Time really is money around here.*

"Um, Ms...." Andre started, realizing he didn't know her last name.

"The name is Candace Narvold, but everyone just calls me Candy," she said pleasantly.

"Thanks," he continued. "Were you here today at one o'clock?"

She nodded. "I was. He was at the luncheon so I delayed my lunch hour until he returned."

"So you saw him return from the luncheon?" Molly asked.

A sly smile crossed her lips. "Yes, I saw him after he arrived back from the luncheon."

"And you're sure of the time?" Andre pressed. "You're certain he was back by one?"

She leaned over the desk and folded her hands. "Detective, I'm quite sure of the time. I was in his office when his cell phone alarm went off. It sounds every day at one to remind him to take his medication."

"What medication is that?"

She eyed them shrewdly. "I don't think that's police business. Is there anything else I can help you with?"

They both shook their heads and headed back down the hallway. Molly glanced at the framed photos that lined the wall, each one depicting the same image—Stan Wertz at the opening of a Hometown Grocery store, preparing to cut a yellow ribbon with an enormous pair of scissors. By the time they reached the elevator she'd lost count at fifteen pictures.

"That's a lot of stores," Andre said. "What do you make of him?"

"He's a cool customer," she said, punching the button. "He showed no emotion and offered no help. Very hard to read."

"Do you think Candy's telling the truth?"

"Do you?"

He glanced back down the hallway at Candy. "I don't know. If she likes her job then I'll bet she'd cover for him, but I think she's telling the truth. Judging from that smile on her face when we asked her where she was at one o'clock, I'd say she was with him in his office. And she wasn't taking dictation."

CHAPTER TWO

Maria pushed the swing higher until her feet rose above her head and her toes seemed to touch the puffy clouds. Back and forth she soared like the pendulum Mrs. Stimson had shown the class. She glanced at the empty swing next to her. Where was Selena? Maria frowned. Maybe her mama wouldn't let her out to play. It was Sunday after all, the Lord's Day. Fortunately Mama believed the Lord got his share in the morning and if she was expected to do chores, then it was okay to play later. She liked Mama's logic.

In the distance a man wriggled through a hole in the playground fence. He was still far away, and she was certain he'd cut to the right toward the abandoned school that towered before her. Her brother Franco told her it was called the drugstore and junkies went there all the time. She and her friends could play on the swings and monkey bars, and no one would bother them but he said never *ever* go inside. She'd kept her promise to him. The old place gave her the creeps.

She missed Franco. He didn't live at home anymore. Mama said he was *muerto* because he ran a gang. But he still saw Maria after school sometimes. He told her she was separate from business, and it wasn't her problem. He loved her no matter what. She still felt bad that Mama didn't get along with him, and Mama would be mad if she knew that he visited her.

The man was close enough now that she could see he wore a hat, sweatshirt and jeans. He didn't walk like a junkie, and he was headed toward her. He stared at his feet as if he didn't notice she was there.

"Time to go," she whispered.

The first rule was always to run when a stranger approached. She slowed the swing and prepared to jump as soon as her feet scraped the ground.

"Hey, little girl, can you help me?" the man called. He was hurrying toward her, waving cash, a smile on his face. "I'll pay you."

She didn't buy it. Franco had warned her about strangers. *None of them are good, hija.*

She jumped and landed in the dirt. When she stood, he was standing before her. There was no point in running now since he could easily catch her. Her gaze went to the twenty dollars in his hand. Maybe he was telling the truth. Maybe Franco was wrong about *some* strangers.

"What do you need, mister?"

He frowned. "I'm very sorry."

Her eyes had been focused on the twenty dollar bill. She didn't notice the barrel of the gun until it was pointed at her.

CHAPTER THREE

The polite ringing of a bell signaled an approaching bicyclist and Ari and Molly veered to the right, allowing him to pass. A couple on a tandem quickly followed behind. The congestion on the cement path was heavy because of the incredible weather, and pedestrians and cyclists jockeyed for a place on the thin thoroughfare that surrounded Tempe Town Lake. While everyone on the eastern seaboard braced for miserable cold fronts that would headline the national news, February in Arizona meant hiking in shorts, driving with the top down and a well-deserved afternoon of relaxation. They'd turned off their cell phones, ensuring that the peaceful Sunday afternoon wouldn't be destroyed by any of Ari's needy real estate clients or cops looking for Molly to run a homicide investigation.

Molly nudged Ari's shoulder with her own. "Hey, where are you?" she asked.

"I'm just amazed by this place," Ari explained. "When you were growing up did you ever think there would be a *lake* here?"

Molly laughed and shook her head. Both of them were Arizona natives and had spent years crossing the Tempe Bridge over the dusty remains of the Salt River, a tributary that had once been a vital waterway at the turn of the century. Built on the perimeter of Tempe, Phoenix's sister city, the lake actually sat in the middle of a riverbed that hadn't seen water in twenty-five years since the great flood of 1980.

As they meandered down the South Bank Path, Molly marveled at the ingenuity of the city planners. The previous mayor who had spearheaded the project was horribly ridiculed by the town council. They'd argued that desert rats didn't understand lakes, and they certainly didn't own boats.

How wrong they were. She glanced at the shimmering blue water and the white sails that floated past. The area around the lake was a developer's dream. Ari and her boss had sold a few parcels of the land used for the upscale apartment complexes that sat west of the lake. Only a lone office building hugged the pathway, its curved blue glass facing the lake and the nearby freeway. To the east a crane rested inside a giant pit, a billboard plastered on the chain link fence surrounding the pit advertising lakefront condos. It was only a matter of time before the area was overdeveloped and the lake became another hub of activity in Tempe.

They strolled on the gravel path, opting to avoid the growing number of cyclists and rollerbladers who inhabited the elevated sidewalk. They turned around at the boat landing and wandered back to Beach Park. Passing under the arch of the Tempe Bridge was eerie, the wheels of the cars overhead chugging along the old ruts of the bridge's lanes. The foot path expanded into the grassy areas of the park and Splash Playground. They found a bench and listened to squeals of glee as rambunctious kids clad in shorts and T-shirts darted in and out of the arching water jets, all the while shivering in the mid-sixties temperatures. Children bounded from water cannons to the small slide disguised inside a large rock and then went to play in the sand nearby.

Molly gazed at Ari, who watched the children intently, amused by their antics. Ari certainly seemed to enjoy kids. When they visited her niece and nephew, Ari was the one who never tired of reading stories, playing baseball or having tea with the dollies. She wondered if Ari wanted a child of her own, a thought she personally couldn't fathom. She'd not mentioned the subject. In fact there were many subjects she'd delicately sidestepped, too petrified to handle emotional intimacy. Physical intimacy was one thing—and with Ari there were no boundaries—but sharing her greatest fears and vulnerabilities was nearly impossible. She kept those buried deep inside a whiskey bottle.

"Hey," Ari whispered, her index finger tracing the side of Molly's jaw. "Now *you* look a million miles away."

"I'm just thinking about the case," she lied. "It's going nowhere. The handwriting analysis was inconclusive, and we haven't found anyone who saw anything, not that it was easy. People don't usually hang out in parking garages, and it's been a nightmare trying to connect with all of the business people who work in the towers next door."

"Did you interview Stan Wertz?"

"Yup. Him and his secretary. She says he was back in the office at one o'clock."

"And you're comfortable that she's telling the truth?"

Molly stroked her cheek. She loved the way that Ari phrased things in such a way that didn't question her professional judgment. She just asked reflective questions. Their conversations had helped her solve a few cases since they'd been together.

"I'm not sure what to believe. After the interview Andre was convinced she's having an affair with him, and they were in the middle of doing it at one o'clock. She says his cell alarm went off and she heard it."

"What about the wife?"

"She's distraught, but the marriage was unstable. Both of them had talked to a divorce attorney recently."

"There's an angle."

Molly nodded in agreement. Most people were killed by people they knew, not strangers, and spouses and lovers accounted for most of the doers.

"It could be but it's looking unlikely. We've spent the week combing through his business affairs, and she doesn't have much of a connection. She claims there was another woman and that was her motivation for the divorce."

"Does she know who it was?"

Molly shook her head. "No. She's still a suspect, but she's the one pushing for the investigation. She says that it wasn't suicide."

"Why?"

"He had too much to live for. The business was doing well, and she didn't recognize the flask."

"Did he ever drink from a flask?"

Molly grinned and nodded. "Sometimes."

Ari shrugged. "So maybe he bought a new one. Was he upset about the divorce?"

"Very upset which is why I haven't ruled out suicide. He was incredibly despondent. They have a nine-one-one call to the house about two weeks ago. He was drunk and screaming at her."

"Anything else in the car or the briefcase?"

"Not really. Just some standard business forms, brochures about his company and the usual stuff you find—mints, Tic Tacs and gum. There was also a key."

Ari raised an eyebrow. "A key? What kind of key?"

"Like a front door key, but it didn't fit the Edgington's front door. It wasn't on a key chain. A couple of those garbage bag twist-ties, a red and white one, were tied to the end, probably so he wouldn't lose it."

"Did you show it to the wife?"

"She'd never seen it. We tried to unlock every door at his home and office with that key and nothing."

She kicked the ground with her shoe, tired of the subject. "Maybe it was a suicide. The coroner's report should be back tomorrow. It'll probably say that he killed himself with booze and pills or somebody planted some poison in that flask. If it's just booze and pills, I know we'll be pulled off the case. Ruskin wants this to go away."

Ari rolled her eyes at the mention of Molly's boss. "Of course he wants it to go away. He wants to clear every case as fast as possible to keep his precious career on track."

They both knew David Ruskin had dreams of replacing Police Chief Sol Gardener, Ari's godfather and her father's best friend.

Ari stretched out her legs, and Molly gazed at her muscular tanned calves. She basked in the sunlight, her eyes closed. She smiled. She could sink into her deep green eyes and dark, shimmering black hair. Ari was beautiful with incredible olive skin and a lean body. Women and men flirted with her on a daily basis, and while she always politely rebuffed their overt advances and proposals for dinner, Molly could tell she enjoyed the attention—she would often flirt back innocently. Today she'd pulled her tresses into a loose bun, some of which had come undone and shrouded her face, the face of a model. Whether she was going to a fancy party or struggling to get out of bed, she was stunning. Every time Molly paused to stare at her, she couldn't take a breath.

"I need a mocha latte," she announced. "Want one?"

Ari nodded, her attention returning to the children's area, while Molly wandered to the nearby coffee bar. She patiently waited in the long line, watching the two energetic college students expertly grind and whip the caffeinated concoctions. Her gaze drifted back to Ari. She could spend hours looking at her. At night when she was fast asleep, Molly would awaken and study her, letting her lips tenderly kiss the slopes of Ari's shoulders.

The goofy smile that covered her face quickly faded when a shapely blonde on rollerblades coasted next to Ari and planted herself on the bench.

Heat burned through her as the woman inched closer to Ari, her arm extended across the back of the bench, her fingers millimeters from Ari's creamy flesh. Ari didn't seem to notice. Nothing about her mannerisms was suggestive or flirtatious. Yet the woman gushed with emotion, laughing heartily at everything she said, her voice drifting across the courtyard and slapping Molly in the face. The box of jealousy that lived next to her heart exploded, and she took two steps out of line. Suddenly her feet stopped, and she almost fell over herself. Ari wouldn't approve—she would be appalled and embarrassed if Molly confronted the woman and shoved her into the lake. It would not be a pleasant way to end their romantic afternoon. She needed to let it go.

Molly turned back to the line, estimating that it would be another five minutes before she returned to the bench with their lattes. By then Ari could have left her, moved in with the blonde and adopted one of the children splashing in the fountain. She closed her eyes and refused to watch the woman's flirtations, determined to let the jealousy ooze away, steeling her fears, reminding herself that Ari's commitment was unwavering and undeniable. The mantra was one she recited often. It disguised the most distasteful aspect of her personality. At least she hoped her raging jealousy wasn't obvious to Ari. She'd never said anything about it, and Molly knew she was an expert at hiding emotions. Yet dealing with her hot-bloodedness cost her dearly, always draining her of energy and leaving her craving a drink.

She paid for the lattes and returned to the bench. The blonde was still seated next to Ari, her skating forgotten. Ari was explaining property values in Tempe while the woman feigned extraordinary interest. Molly smiled broadly as the blonde's face crumbled when she settled next to Ari, handed her the latte and wrapped a possessive arm around *her* woman. The rollerblader recognized her deep cleavage and short shorts were being wasted on Ari, who obliviously continued to ramble on about mortgage rates. When she unconsciously snuggled up against Molly, the blonde leaned forward, attempting an exit.

"Hey, it's been nice talking to you," she said, interrupting her mid-sentence, "but I've got to cruise. See you around, Ari."

And without waiting for a reply the woman skated toward Mill Avenue. Ari wiped the puzzled expression from her face and took a sip of the coffee. "Weird," was her only comment.

"Who was that?" Molly asked innocently.

"Deandra, or something like that," she replied absently, her eyes returning to the children.

Molly squeezed her shoulder and they drank their lattes in silence, basking in the mild winter weather, envying the lives of the children who had no cares or worries. Ari laughed as one child turned the water cannon on her older brother, spraying him in the chest, screaming with delight. The older boy yelled at his sister and chased her around the park. When an airplane roared overhead, preparing to land at the airport that sat between Phoenix and Tempe, the children froze and looked up. A few pointed and all were mesmerized.

"What time are you picking up your dad?" Molly asked, the sight of the airplane reminding her of Ari's afternoon plans.

Ari sighed. "About three. We'll probably go have a late lunch before I drop him off at Sol's."

"Do you want me to come with you?"

It was a question Molly had wanted to ask all week but had avoided because she knew the answer—no. As much as she wanted to meet Big Jack Adams and as much as she knew it would help her deal with the growing commitment she felt toward Ari, she knew Ari had too much history with her father—bad history—to bring a girlfriend into the picture. He'd disowned her years ago when he learned she was gay, she'd tried to commit suicide, his wife had divorced him before her death, and it had taken four years for this reunion to occur.

She offered a withered look and Molly kissed her forehead. "I understand. It's okay." *But it still hurts.*

Ari stared at the elevator and made no effort to press the call button. A screech of tires made her jump, and she glanced toward a car speeding up the spiral ramp to the next level of the parking garage. While they were in a hurry, she moved in slow motion, dreading the next few hours. The elevator suddenly chimed and the doors opened. Passengers hustled out and she boarded, knowing it was a sign.

As the elevator descended an odd sensation overtook her. It was as if a string was pulling her closer to the past and this reunion with her father. She checked her watch, thinking he'd probably deplaned by now and was waiting by security, the place where they'd agreed to meet.

It was one of many agreements. She would pick him up, and they would have a late lunch but there was nothing else planned for Sunday. He wouldn't stay with her but at Sol's. If the lunch went well, they might go to dinner, but they had to agree. Eventually he might meet Molly. She hadn't said anything to him about having a girlfriend. She knew, though, that their paths would inevitably cross at the police station.

She headed for the security area, but he wasn't there. She moved underneath the TV monitors and saw that his plane had arrived half an hour early. She stationed herself against a wall so she would see him when he passed the checkpoint. Maybe he was in one of the gift stores along the D concourse.

A familiar belly laugh erupted from the security area and her gaze settled on a group of TSA workers clustered around Jack Adams.

He towered over all of them and gave one of the young guys a pat on the shoulder. Dressed in a blue button-down oxford shirt, tweed blazer and jeans, Jack looked forty-five and not fifty-eight. Ari knew her good genes were a blessing from both of her parents, although she was nearly a mirror image of her dead mother Lucia.

How he'd managed to get into the sacred security area was a mystery, but Ari wasn't surprised. He could charm anyone—his good looks made women swoon and men jealous. He looked up beyond the waiting passengers and their eyes met. She felt no urge to wave or smile but he did. He pointed to her and soon the TSA workers were staring as well. He grabbed his carry-on and waved good-bye to his new friends.

Before she could jam her hands into her pockets and avoid a hug, he wrapped his massive arms around her and she was compelled to return the gesture. Fortunately he pulled away quickly, still holding her shoulders with his huge hands.

"You are absolutely beautiful," he said. "Just like your mom."

At the mention of her mother, her lip began to quiver. She looked away, her eyes welling with tears. "Um, Dad—"

"No, no," he said, handing her a tissue from his pocket. "There will be none of that. You're supposed to be angry with me, not sad. When someone's an asshole, you don't cry about it, do you?"

She couldn't help but laugh. *He always knows how to break*

the tension. "Let's get your bags," she said, turning toward the escalator.

Conversation proved unnecessary as they collected his giant duffle and made their way to the car. The general commotion surrounding the task and his inherent nature to chat with anyone around him excused her from discussing the list of mundane topics she'd committed to memory on her way to the airport. Instead he resumed a conversation with an elderly woman he must have met on the plane and on their way up to the garage, he turned to a man next to him and asked, "Is Durant's still the best place in town to get a steak?"

The man said yes, but other passengers disagreed and a short but lively discussion ensued. It was the noisiest elevator ride she'd ever endured. Once they were in the 4Runner and driving away, she mentally reviewed her topic list.

"I don't want to talk about the weather, the Diamondbacks or how much the valley has changed in the last four years," he said suddenly, interrupting her thoughts. "What else is there?"

She shook her head and a sliver of a smile crossed her lips. She didn't want to like him again. "You've just vetoed all the easy ones, Dad, so you pick."

"Let's talk about Jane."

She chuckled, knowing her best friend was great conversation material. A fellow real estate agent, he'd known Jane Frank for years.

"Good choice," she agreed. "Jane's doing great, making lots of money and continuing her quest for the perfect woman."

"I take it the quest may be never ending?"

She shook her head and merged with the freeway traffic. "Jane is a free spirit. She loves being single."

"Do you?"

Her mouth went dry. She knew that if she looked over at him, one eyebrow would be arched, his head would be lowered and he would be peering over the top of his sunglasses. She focused intently on the Saab in front of her and didn't answer right away. She finally said, "I think we need to talk about something else."

He sighed and looked out the window. "Fine."

Neither said anything else until she pulled into a parking spot outside of McGurkee's Sandwich Shop.

He shifted in his seat and in an excited voice blurted, "How 'bout those Phoenix Suns?"

CHAPTER FOUR

Twilight slipped over the McDowell Mountains as he entered the preserve. He followed the strip of asphalt around several curves, past the picnic ramadas and parking areas that lined the road. Remnants of Saturday night parties lay discarded along the desert embankment—fast food wrappers, soda cans and dozens of beer bottles. The piles of trash grew thick at the base of the ramadas, the sanctified places of congregation. He shook his head at human thoughtlessness and avoided the glass shards that littered the roadway.

As a cop he knew the police view: if no one called to complain and nobody got shot, desert parties were ignored. It was the line between violence and revelry—a fine line at best—but the lack of police manpower made the distinction necessary.

He scowled as a cloud of dust enveloped his car, worrying

that the dirt path would ruin his suspension. The road crested over a hill. He saw the ramada and a dark Explorer parked next to it. Behind the wheel, Vince Carnotti, the leader of the Carnotti crime family, a known felon and his surreptitious boss, spoke into his cell phone.

He pulled up behind the Explorer and quickly joined him. He nodded at Carnotti, a man who was twice his size with enormous hands. He was rumored to have crushed a man's skull just by putting his head in a vice grip.

He waited until Carnotti slapped his phone shut and asked, "How are you, Vince?" He tried to sound casual but noticed the slight quake in his voice.

Carnotti nodded slowly. "I'm good. The weather helps my joints. I can't stand New York winters anymore, but this fuckin' inversion layer drives my emphysema crazy."

"I hear you, Vince."

Carnotti turned in his seat and pointed. "What are we doin' about that dyke, Molly Nelson?"

He nodded, grateful that Carnotti moved right to business. "It's handled." He hoped he sounded confident but not cocky.

"I'm trusting you," Carnotti said. "Nelson got too close to our operation during that whole Itchy Moon thing. You of all people should know what we stand to lose."

"I'm well aware of what's at stake," he said.

He would be the first to die, or worse, go to prison if the operation was exposed. The media would crucify him as a dirty cop, and his family would pay the price. But he was in too far to go back.

He added, "Really, Vince, you don't need to worry. I'm working another angle. Believe me, I know her weak points and how to exploit them. By the time I'm through her career will be history."

CHAPTER FIVE

Molly sipped her scotch, wondering how Ari's reunion with her father was going. She really understood her dilemma but wanted to connect with Captain Big Jack Adams, a retired cop who hated her current boss almost as much as she did.

She rubbed her eyes and stared at the spreadsheets she'd set on the bar. The numbers seemed to blur together, and she blinked several times to clear her head. All of the entries began with 6815, four numbers she was sure were part of an address, the address of a mole in the police department—a person who'd had her informant decapitated and stuffed in a trunk. She'd combed the list of owners many times looking for a clue, but so far none of the individual names or corporations stood out. *It might help if you weren't drinking in a bar.*

She drained her second scotch and motioned to Vicky.

Vicky poured another round, her eyebrow raised. "This is a little early for you, Molly."

"Who are you? My AA sponsor?"

Vicky shook her head and walked away. It was their latest running joke. Vicky was the only person allowed to comment on her drinking. Not even Ari said anything. She understood it was a taboo topic, but Molly imagined if she knew that she was frequenting Hideaway nearly every day, she would vehemently object. She'd also be crushed if she learned that her increased drinking coincided with their recent declaration of love and commitment.

She gulped her drink and stared into the empty glass. She loved Ari. She knew that. But she couldn't understand how a woman with the body of a goddess would want a woman built like a linebacker. She lived in fear that Ari would someday ask herself the same question. Yet after eight months Ari remained.

Her cell phone chirped, and she frowned when she saw that it was Andre. Why would he be calling on Sunday?

"What's up?"

"We're working, Mol. It's a big case and Ruskin's asking for us. Says Sol Gardener called us in." The excitement in his voice was unmistakable.

David Ruskin was their boss, and the only reason he would ever request her would be because he was directed to do so by the chief of police.

"What's the case?"

"Ten-year-old girl shot at Washington School."

Molly was confused. "What about the Edgington murder?"

"Coroner ruled it a suicide, and now we've got this case. I'm on my way to the crime scene. Get your ass down here!"

Washington School stood like an old watchman over South Phoenix. Built in 1917, the school was a throwback to the east coast design, a single rectangular building with two stories. Rows of parallel windows wrapped around the entire structure and a set of steep concrete stairs led up to the enormous front doors.

Molly and Andre stared at the façade. The majesty it possessed in past decades had vanished. Every window pane was riddled with holes from rocks or bullets. The thousands of tan bricks lining the exterior were faded from the unforgiving Arizona sun.

A dozen crime techs and officers scoured the grounds as they walked across the dusty remnants of the schoolyard, patches of hardy Bermuda grass still visible and kept alive by the intermittent rains.

Andre's gaze swept the property. "When did they close this place?"

She shook her head. "I don't know. A long time ago. And now it just sits here."

They stopped in front of the swing set, the crime scene tape loosely draped around the poles in haphazard fashion. A tarp rested over the body, and Andre squatted, lifting up a corner while she turned away. She hated looking at dead kids. She stared at the swing, wondering if the little girl had been terrified or if she'd known her killer and death was just an unexpected moment free of fear. She sucked in her breath as a wave of nausea passed through her. She closed her eyes, wishing she was back at Hideaway.

"Tell me what we know."

"Victim is Maria Perez. She was found in front of the swings. There's a dirt scrape here that suggests she was trying to stop the swing—"

"Because she was going to run away," she added.

He nodded. "Maybe. It's hard to know. Shot at point-blank range with a thirty-eight. Took one bullet to the chest and fell to the ground. Found around five by two teenagers coming to make out on that bench over there."

They walked the twenty feet to the bench. It was old, and she couldn't imagine anyone sitting on the rotten wood. Yet the ground was littered with condom wrappers, suggesting that more than kissing occurred on the warped planks.

"Are the techs searching the school?" she asked, her gaze settling on the two end rows of windows, the ones facing the playground.

"Yeah, but so far they haven't found anything. Not that it would be easy. The place is a mess. Tons of trash everywhere, vermin and bugs. There wasn't anything obvious."

"Obvious," she repeated. "Let's go across the grounds first."

Andre read from his notes. "The teenagers told the first officer that everybody knows to stay away from the school. That's for the drug users only. I guess the kids play on the equipment, and the addicts leave the kids alone, sort of an unspoken rule."

They silently walked the perimeter, going around the long way. He pointed at a piece of fence ripped away from its post. Judging from its location, it was an entry for drug users, away from the street, away from patrol cars. Only a zealous cop, one who wanted to go looking for trouble, would bother to get out and inspect the area on foot, which was unlikely to happen very often.

They rounded the backside of the building, and she saw a second hole, the one the children used. She realized the school sat on a huge plot of land, and indeed it would be possible for the addicts and street people to enter through the east side of the fence and never know there were children to the west of the building. She doubted the two groups came in contact, but perhaps they had yesterday.

They headed toward the school as the last crime tech exited with a shake of his head toward Andre. Molly scowled, almost certain they'd missed a clue. Her gut told her there was something inside. She was sure of it.

The smell assaulted her as she crossed the threshold. She immediately shone her flashlight at her feet, worried that she'd step in excrement or a rat would scurry across her loafer. The path in front of her was clear, but trash and drug paraphernalia lined the walls. She imagined the classrooms were equally disgusting if not worse. They stepped into the first room they came to, the winter sun already struggling to set. A weak light seeped across the floor, the filthy windows obscuring the brightness she'd hoped to find.

"This is practically hopeless today," she murmured. "We need to come back tomorrow."

"Can't we do it now," he whined.

She threw him a glare. She knew he hated to get dirty. "Quit being such a princess."

CHAPTER SIX

Ari floated on the edge of consciousness unable to decide whether to rise and get an early start on what would likely be a hectic Monday or stay in bed for another half hour, avoiding the inevitable beginning of the week. Her head sunk deeper into the soft pillow, making the decision for her, and she reached for the comforter, longing to cocoon herself in the soft down.

Molly had other plans and pulled all the covers away. She wrapped her arms around her and caressed her nipples.

"Yes, my love," Ari whispered.

She sighed, caught between the gentle touch of Molly's lips as they lazily explored her earlobe and the very deliberate motions of Molly's fingers, nestled between her legs in maddening foreplay.

"Let go," Molly commanded and Ari felt her mind float away in the morning sunlight.

When she stopped quaking twenty minutes later, Molly's hand drifted over the curves of her legs and bare bottom. "You have the most beautiful body," she said. "I hope I please you."

"Uh-huh. That was magnificent."

Molly smiled at the compliment, but Ari knew her answer wouldn't matter. She had come to realize that bolstering Molly's confidence was a requirement of their relationship—regardless of what she said, Molly doubted her. Ari would never understand the sexual power she wielded over her. When Molly touched her she lost all control, her body responding with animal instincts to each caress.

Swatting her buttocks playfully, Molly rose from the bed and disappeared into the living room. She smiled as the steady rhythm of piano notes filled the small apartment. Some women enjoyed the afterglow of sex in each other's arms, but she was serenaded by her lover, an accomplished pianist who played for very few people and was composing a song, *Aria*, just for her. It was the most intimate and romantic gesture she could have ever imagined, knowing Molly poured her creative genius into a gift unlike any other.

The familiar music drifted into random notes like an unfinished road disappearing abruptly into the forest. She experimented with various chords and replayed changes until the road extended a little further than before. Her ability to evaluate her music amazed Ari. She would construct musical riffs, connecting some to the piece and throwing the others out, a kind of musical trash. Eventually she returned to the beginning and played what she had written so far.

No longer willing to lounge in bed alone, Ari rose and wandered to the living room. Sunlight seeped through the closed blinds casting shadows over the black piano. Molly's naked body swayed gently back and forth, her shoulders rising and falling with the music. Ari hovered and explored her tangled, blond curls.

Molly continued to play, albeit poorly, despite her touch. She leaned back and Ari enveloped her in a full embrace, her lips taking up residence at the base of her neck.

"Oh, God," Molly sighed. Her arched fingers collapsed on the ivory keys, announcing her willing defeat.

Ari tipped her chin and buried her tongue deep in her mouth while her hands fondled the large breasts she dearly loved. She ended the kiss and stared into her blue eyes. Molly radiated beauty and intelligence even if she didn't know it.

"Let's go back to bed," Ari said, a wicked smile on her face. "I believe I owe you an incredible orgasm."

"I can't," she groaned. "I have to get to work early. We need to interview Maria Perez's mother and go back to the crime scene. It was nearly dark last night, and I'm worried we missed something."

Molly wandered into the bathroom and Ari's ever curious nature demanded that she follow. "What happened to the Edgington case?"

She shook her head. "Apparently it wasn't a murder. Coroner says the guy killed himself with booze and pills mixed in the flask."

She remembered the silver flask next to Edgington, the scrawled note and the locked door. It certainly looked like a suicide.

"Were his fingerprints on the note?"

Molly grinned. "I love it when you think like a cop." She kissed her forehead and stepped into the shower. "Yup, his fingerprints were on it." She kissed her again and shut the curtain. "Suicide, babe," she said over the whoosh of the shower spray.

Ari frowned. She'd met Warren Edgington, and he hadn't acted suicidal. He'd flirted shamelessly like a man about to be divorced and free.

She opened the shower curtain and gazed at Molly's incredible body. "You know, they're both involved in real estate."

"That's not a motive, honey, so now Andre and I get to investigate the murder of a kid. Shot in the heart at close range."

She turned away and busied herself with the soap. While Molly would never have children of her own, she loved them, particularly her niece and nephew, who adored her and welcomed Ari as their second aunt. This was a horrible case to inherit.

Molly glanced up and said, "Honey, I need to get ready, and as much as I love shower sex, I just can't today."

Ari nodded and retreated to the bedroom, feeling a door close between them. Lately more and more doors seemed to close, and she didn't know why. She had thought that once they declared their love Molly's anxieties would lessen, but often she seemed more uncomfortable whenever they talked about love. She'd told her she needed more time and all Ari could do now was be patient. But once in a while, when she thought of the future, Molly wasn't there.

She pushed the doubts from her mind and reached for her cell phone, neglected for the last twelve hours. She had five messages—from Jane, two clients, her father and Lorraine. Feeling slightly guilty over missing Lorraine's call, she quickly punched the speed dial.

"Hola, chica."

"Hey, Lorraine. What's going on?"

"When are you coming in? I've got big plans for us today."

"I should be there in an hour. I've got to stop by my place and change."

"Does this mean you got some quality time with the detective this weekend?"

Ari smiled. It was so nice to work for someone who didn't care that her lover was a woman. "It does. We spent half of Sunday together."

"Good for you. Okay, I'll see you when you get here. 'Bye."

"Wait!" Ari blurted. "You can't leave me in suspense. What's the big news?"

"Only the greatest deal of your life."

She pulled into the driveway of Southwest Realty, parking behind Lorraine's Lexus. A converted bungalow from the 1920s, Lorraine had bought the run-down property for a song, refurbished the entire interior and established her business in an area of town that few saw as having any promise, including her family who lived a mile away.

Ari's office was a guest room in the house's previous life, with two beautiful picture windows that welcomed sunlight against the brightly painted yellow walls. She dropped her briefcase on the antique desk and pulled up the blinds.

"Good morning, chica!"

Lorraine popped her head in the doorway. She sported her usual tailored suit that accentuated her curvy figure and fine jewelry that matched perfectly. She was elegant and Jane lusted after her regularly—much to her delight.

"Sorry I'm late."

She shook her head. "You're not late. In fact you're just in time." She checked her watch. "We need to go in a few minutes. Get yourself organized and grab a coffee if you want. I'll fill you in while we drive."

She disappeared and Ari tackled the contents of her briefcase. She withdrew the files she'd finished on Saturday and arranged them alphabetically on her desk by client name. She attached sticky notes to paperwork that still needed her attention, and she sighed with relief as she stuck a file into her out basket, for it meant that a deal had closed and she could expect a check soon. Her cell phone chirped just as she was organizing her to-do list for the day. She didn't need to check the caller ID to know it was Jane.

"Hey Janie."

"Let me guess. It's nine forty-two, so you've just finished prioritizing your phone messages, right? Or have you redone your entire filing system? Perhaps you've solved the issue of world peace?"

She laughed. "Even I couldn't handle that before noon."

"Why was your phone off last night? You should never turn it off."

She blushed at the thought of her cell phone ringing during her passionate evening with Molly. It would have entirely ruined the mood. "I wasn't accepting calls," she said simply.

"Oh, so you and your girlfriend were incognito. I see. I'll never understand you, Ari."

"What? Don't you ever turn off your cell?"

"No, I don't. You never know when you'll miss a deal. But that's not what I'm talking about. I'll never understand the girlfriend part."

She could hear the disapproval in Jane's voice. "Not all of us like the free life, honey."

"I know. You and Molly are destined for each other."

She sighed. "I don't know about that. It seems lately we aren't communicating very well."

"What are you talking about?"

"Ever since we said the L word it's been more difficult, or at least it seems that way. Every time I say I love her she tenses up, and her face freezes like I'm telling her about a plane crash."

Jane chuckled. "Honey, you're being a little dramatic."

"I know." She noticed some stray specks of dust on her blotter and reached for a tissue. "So what's up? You need to talk fast because we're heading out in a few minutes."

"Where are you going?"

"I don't know. She's being very mysterious."

"Sounds potentially lucrative. Well, I just wanted to call and see how the reunion went with your father. Did the two of you make up?"

She smiled at Jane's simplistic view of the world where every problem should be solved immediately or no longer than it took to work out in a thirty-minute television show. "We made a start. We're going to have dinner tonight. Can you come?"

"No. I'd love to play Switzerland, but I've got a hot date."

"With whom?"

"Oh, just someone I met online."

She closed her eyes. Jane knew enough women without meeting more in cyberspace. She had recently brushed against death because of her loose ways.

"Don't tell me that you've started dating online."

"No, no. This is just a friend and maybe a potential client. Gotta go."

Before Ari could comment Jane disconnected. She frowned and cradled the receiver. Jane didn't have any true female friends except her. Everyone else was a conquest, business associate or potential lover.

"Ari, let's go!" Lorraine called.

She quickly grabbed her bag and headed out the door. Jane

would do whatever she wanted, and Ari would inevitably pick up the pieces.

Ari followed Lorraine's directions into the Day Arbor neighborhood, one of the most prestigious historic districts in the heart of Central Phoenix. Day Arbor offered eclectic architecture, sprawling lawns and unique floor plans that featured dumbwaiters and secret passageways. The fact that the neighborhood sat next to a golf course only added to its appeal.

They drove through the secluded residential streets until Lorraine directed her to stop in front of an incredible two-story Spanish colonial revival, and in Ari's opinion, the nicest house on the block. The recently clipped grass and hedges nestled against the ground floor windows were trimmed perfectly straight. A Romeo and Juliet balcony perched over the mature chili pepper trees which dotted the yard and a red brick walk trailed through the plush Bermuda to an emerald green front door.

"A new listing?" she asked, following behind Lorraine, studying every inch of the house in admiration.

"We'll see," Lorraine said with a grin. "You remember Stan Wertz from that terrible luncheon?"

She rolled her eyes and sighed. "You've got to be kidding. He hit on me."

Lorraine held up her hands. "Listen, chica, I know it's not right. He's probably a sexual harasser, but this is big money and I know we'll get the buyer's *and* seller's commissions if we work it together. Sweetie, we're talking a six figure commission potentially."

She gritted her teeth. There was more to life than money, but she could definitely endure a little butt-leering and ogling if it meant that *much* money.

"Fine."

A woman in a crisp grey uniform answered their ring. The turned-up lace cuffs of her short sleeves matched the apron that she wore. She was an older Hispanic woman who tried to hide her tired eyes behind a cordial expression.

"May I help you?"

Lorraine flashed her ultimate power smile. "Absolutely. And you are…?" She stuck her hand out in greeting, and the woman graciously took it, obviously a bit surprised that a guest would actually introduce herself.

"I'm Dora, Mr. Wertz's domestic."

Ari suppressed a giggle at the expressions of the rich. She looked back down the street and wondered if everyone had a *domestic*.

Lorraine continued to shake the woman's hand furiously. "I'm Lorraine Gonzalez and this is my associate Ari Adams. We have an appointment with Mr. Wertz."

"Please come in." Dora gestured toward the long entryway.

Ari lingered behind, admiring the antiques and wall hangings that surrounded them. Her jaw dropped as she passed what she thought might be a real Chagall, but Lorraine never commented. They stepped through an archway as she noticed the amazing patterns embedded in the tile—the reds, turquoises and browns swirling in a bold circular design. Dora deposited them in the living room and Ari marveled at the stained glass window across the room. The place was highly inviting, its wooden beams spanning the cathedral ceiling.

"I smell money," Lorraine whispered.

She chuckled as clipped heels drew closer. Stan Wertz emerged through another archway carrying a putter over his shoulder. He was dressed in golf shorts and a polo shirt, a white visor with a designer logo hiding much of his black and silver hair. He epitomized a rich, powerful man, and she found herself slightly intimidated in his presence. Lorraine on the other hand seemed entirely at ease. Ari found it ironic that a woman who had grown up with nothing so easily acclimated to another social class.

"Mr. Wertz," Lorraine gushed, "It's wonderful to see you again. I'm sure you remember my associate Ari Adams."

"Absolutely."

He dropped her handshake quickly as his eyes settled on Ari's figure. He held her fingers longer than necessary, and she understood why Lorraine wanted her there. She would close the deal—or rather her looks would help ensure that by the time they left, a Southwest Realty sign would be sitting in his driveway ready for the post to be placed in his yard.

"I'm so glad you called me. I'd love to show you what we can do. I know we can move your house quickly," she added.

At the mention of a quick sale his glance shifted back to her. "And what would *you* do to sell my house fast?" he asked skeptically.

Ari doubted they were the first agents he'd interviewed.

Lorraine smiled broadly and looked around. "A house like this sells itself. We just have to give it the right PR—an open house, a mailing, some phone calls to key buyers that I know and most importantly a well-worded listing in the service."

He seemed impressed by her confidence and nodded his head in agreement.

"Why don't you show us around?" she suggested.

"Of course," he said, dropping the putter into a corner and leading them to the back of the house. Ari lost her breath as they entered a solarium. Her eyes were immediately drawn to the southern exposure, the source of light for the entire room. Large beveled glass panes stood side by side, affording an exceptional view of the lush backyard. A window seat ran the length of the wall, and she pictured herself curling up with a good book. She would have quite a selection of titles from which to choose since the adjoining wall housed rows of books in the floor-to-ceiling built-in shelves. Couches and chaise lounges were scattered about, creating conversation niches that would be perfect for a party. A Steinway grand piano sat in a corner away from the direct sunlight. She immediately thought how much Molly would love this space.

"What an exceptional room," Lorraine gushed. "It has so many uses."

He snorted. "This was my wife's. She insisted we buy that monstrosity," he said, pointing at the piano, "and then she never played. After she left I'd thought about turning the place into a game room, but I'm rarely home."

Lorraine shook her head. "That's too bad. I'm sure you could use the relaxation. I can't imagine how hard it must be to run a grocery store chain."

"I've always got to stay ahead," he said as they moved back down the hall.

Ari lingered in the solarium a moment longer, gazing at the piano. She crossed the living room and entered the den which reeked of macho man. A plasma TV covered one wall and animal heads stared at each other from around the room. A poker table sat in a corner and Ari could smell the faint odor of cigars. She blinked twice before she understood the setup in the opposite corner. Parquet flooring and stage lighting illuminated a long slender pole that extended from ceiling to floor.

"Unbelievable," she muttered in disgust.

Of course the room wouldn't be complete without a fancy bar—the array of liquor suggested Wertz could create any drink ordered. She noticed a decorative shelf lining the top of the bar. He'd chosen to display a collection of antique bottles and flasks, and she noticed one that looked quite similar to the silver flask found inside Warren Edgington's car.

"Ari, where are you?" Lorraine called. "We're going upstairs."

She tore her gaze away from the flasks and found them at the base of a winding staircase. They climbed to an open loft that Ari thought would be a great office space. The two second floor bedrooms were contemporary, painted in rich earth tones with deep rust accents around the windows. The floors had been redone in bamboo, her favorite look. By the time they returned to the living room, she was in love with the home and wondered how she could afford a seven-figure price tag.

"So how much can you get for my house?" he asked.

"We can do well, Stan. I know you want top dollar, but the house must appraise," she said plainly. "I've done a comparative market analysis, and I'm sure we could get over a million."

Ari listened as Lorraine explained the role of the seller's agent, keeping her eyes squarely on her boss. She knew he was staring at her despite Lorraine's efforts to engage him in conversation. He interrupted twice to ask questions, but when she presented the contract to him, he signed and initialed at the appropriate places, not bothering to read the ten pages of small print.

"So, now what?" he asked.

"I'll put it in the listing system as soon as we get back to the office," she assured him. "I imagine that you'll have an offer soon."

"I hope so. I'm dying to get rid of this place. I've fallen in love with golf, and I've got my eye on Desert Mountain."

She joined in his enthusiasm, clearly sensing an opportunity to help him find his next home. "Without a doubt that's the premier spot," she agreed. "Have you played Verde Lobo?"

He nodded, a huge grin spreading across his face, the expression of a golf junkie. "My favorite is Desert Vista."

She laughed. "Johnny Wilson, the club manager, is a personal friend so let me know if you ever need a favor. I'd be happy to look up listings for you as well."

His eyes shifted to Ari. "Actually, Lorraine, I want you to devote your entire attention to removing this albatross from my back. I was hoping Ari would act as my buyer's agent. What do you say, Ari?"

"Sure," she replied slowly.

Although he was incredibly distasteful, the paycheck would be worth enduring several hours with him as they drove around in her SUV previewing houses. She'd investigate the area thoroughly and hopefully they would find something quickly.

He walked them to the door and took her hand. "I'm looking forward to working with you. Both of you," he quickly added for Lorraine's benefit.

Ari nodded weakly before he closed the enormous front door.

"I think I need a shower," she murmured.

CHAPTER SEVEN

Molly motored through the most depressed residential area of the city. Once the urban center of the valley, South Phoenix harbored the most notorious gangs, served as the epicenter for crack houses and sheltered the city's poor, the majority of whom were Hispanic. Most Phoenicians only saw South Phoenix from the inside of their cars as they motored down I-10 or SR-202, gaining a bird's eye view of the decrepit houses and rundown backyards that stretched across the landscape to the base of South Mountain.

She handed a steaming cup of coffee to Andre, who pored over her spreadsheets looking for the answer to mystery of 6815. Since he had a minor in finance he stood the best chance of finding the answer.

"I've checked out at least fifty of the addresses and nothing jumps out. They all seem legit." He tossed the spreadsheets onto the floor and sipped the coffee. "You know, Mol, I'm happy to help, but you need to realize that if these numbers are an address, whoever owns the place has probably hidden it really well behind shell corporations and false names. We may look right past the answer and not know it."

She nodded. "I get that. But the idea of a dirty cop makes my stomach turn."

"I hear ya."

She slowed as she passed a group of children playing in one of the dirt front yards. No foliage grew anywhere, the residents unable to squander precious water on landscaping. Large trees planted after the Depression once inhabited all of the yards, but when the neighborhoods spiraled downward, the trees like everything else went untended and eventually met a whirring chainsaw. The owners passed the ramshackle places from heir to heir, each one caught on the economic downslide and unable to make any improvements to the property.

"Reminds me of Philly," Andre said. "We had a ton of neighborhoods like this."

"It makes me want to cry," Molly added.

She turned right on Eighth Street and entered a media circus. TV vans lined the sides of the road while reporters and cameramen clustered in front of a drab house and searched for the best shot. The muted green paint had faded from the masonry block, revealing patches of a dusty rose underneath. *Probably the original color from sixty years ago.*

She pulled up in front of a fire hydrant, something a news crew wouldn't dare do. A strip of red against the house caught her eye. It was one of those festive flags people hung on their porch that celebrated or honored nothing but proclaimed cheerfulness about the owners. Emblazoned with a yellow daisy, the banner wasn't the only noticeable difference that separated this house from those of its neighbors. Someone had attempted to create order from chaos—all of the toys and bikes were lined up neatly near the porch.

"What do we know about the family?" she asked.

He scanned the information clipped inside the brown

folder. "Mother is Juanita Perez. Father unknown. Two younger siblings... Whoa. Mol, her older brother is Franco Perez, the leader of Westside Knights."

"Isn't that the gang involved in the big rivalry?"

"Oh, yeah. The Knights are in a turf war with Mayhem Locos, the gang led by Hector Cervantes. These are bad guys, and they'll be happy to die for this little bit of area."

Andre closed the file and reached for the door handle. "That's just great. We're probably in the middle of a gang shooting. Ready to meet the press?"

Molly snorted and kept her eyes focused on the front door, ignoring the microphones and bellowing voices of the reporters. They approached the solid security screen door that kept the Perez's safely between their home and the street. Wrought iron bars covered all of the windows and three gold deadbolts shone against the worn wooden door.

"These people are serious about protecting themselves," he said as he pressed the old buzzer.

"If you lived in this neighborhood, wouldn't you be?"

He shrugged. "There's crime everywhere, not just where poor people live."

She remained silent. She knew he'd grown up in the Philadelphia projects while she'd spent her whole life in the suburbs of predominantly white Phoenix. She kept quiet about racial issues and poverty, and he knew not to expound upon gay rights. They each respected the other's area of expertise.

The door swung open and Molly found herself staring at a silhouette, unable to discern any physical features of the person inside. She held out her shield and hoped she was staring into the woman's eyes.

"Mrs. Perez? I'm Detective Nelson and this is Detective Williams. We're here to talk to you about Maria."

"I've already talked to the police."

"Ma'am, I'm sorry to ask you these questions again, but we're the lead detectives on the case," Andre explained. "We'll try to be fast. We really want to hear all of the details from you."

"It's very important that we get to know Maria," Molly added.

"Come in," she said wearily.

She opened the door and stepped aside. No toys were strewn around the carpet and although the sofa and matching chair were quite worn, they were free of stains and holes. A few family photos dotted the walls but it was evident their money didn't go toward home décor. Yet there was not a speck of obvious dust anywhere.

"We're so sorry about what happened," Molly said.

Mrs. Perez nodded, her lips pursed, as if she was trying not to cry. She motioned to the sofa. She was a large woman who looked much older than her listed age of thirty-seven. This could be me, Molly thought, as her thirty-seventh birthday loomed around the corner. She couldn't imagine what it would be like to be so tired, and she certainly couldn't fathom how anyone could deal with the death of a child.

The sofa faced an old television console. Perched on top were two pictures, a framed school photo of Maria and a candid shot of a teenage boy holding a pre-school aged Maria in his arms and tickling her. The picture conveyed the love of a brother and a sister, the protectiveness of an older sibling toward a younger one. Molly's gaze drifted back to the school photo. Maria wore a blue polo knit shirt and hair in pigtails, but Molly's attention was drawn to the girl's eyes, full of fire and strength. Her broad smile minus a few teeth suggested a mischievous nature. No doubt she was a handful.

As if reading her mind, Andre pointed at the photo. "Is that recent, Ma'am?"

Mrs. Perez rose as if it were the greatest of chores and retrieved the picture. She sat back down and lovingly stroked the sides of the frame. "This was taken last spring at the end of fourth grade. She hated that school uniform. Said that people shouldn't have to dress alike if they didn't want to." Her hands tightened around the cheap wooden border, and she began to sob. "She was only ten years old! How could anyone shoot a child in cold blood?"

Molly waited for her to compose herself before she said, "Let's start with where she was found, the playground at Washington School. Did she go there often?"

"All the kids went there. I don't know what this ridiculous city was thinking. They leave an old empty school standing, but they don't take away the swings and the monkey bars? That's just an invitation to children. And once the neighborhood junkies cut a hole in the fence anyone could get inside."

"So a lot of people come and go?" Andre asked.

Mrs. Perez huffed, "That place is like a motel. It's always open. The cops can't keep the junkies from hiding in the classrooms and doing their drugs while the kids play outside. What's worse is that nobody can tear it down because it's *historic*."

Molly noted the sarcasm in her voice. "Have the police ever intervened?"

She found it hard to believe that the beat cops would tolerate such blatant disregard for the law.

"Oh, they're always driving by, but it's not like anyone's standing outside holding up their crack cocaine for inspection."

Molly made a note to contact the nearby precinct. "Did you worry about Maria going over there?"

Her eyes narrowed. "I know what you're thinking. What kind of mother would let her child hang out with druggies? Believe it or not there was never a problem. It's the only place that's close, and the playground was in the far field away from the main building. No one ever bothered the kids, at least not until now." She started to sob quietly while they waited patiently. Finally she raised her blurry eyes and nodded. "Go on."

"Why don't you tell us about that day," Molly suggested. "Start with when you last saw your daughter."

"She left about eleven. Since it was Sunday she didn't have many chores after church so when she asked if she could go to the playground, I let her."

"And that was around eleven?" Andre confirmed.

"Yes." Her eyes flooded with tears that she willed away. "I never saw her again. All I remember was that little voice saying, 'Adios, Mama, see you in an hour.'"

Molly touched her arm. "I only have a few more questions. I just need to know if you can think of anyone who might want to harm Maria or if she'd talked about having problems with anybody."

She shook her head, a slight smile on her lips. "She was stubborn, always questioning authority. If she didn't like the explanation then she'd do what she pleased. I've got two other children, but Maria gave me all of my gray hair."

She sighed deeply and melted into the sofa. Molly was looking at a broken woman.

Andre coughed. "Ma'am, you mentioned two other children but don't you have three?"

Color rose in her cheeks and she sat straight up on the couch. "That boy, Franco, I don't claim him. He's muerto! Selling drugs, hurting people. I threw him out two years ago, and I haven't seen him since. He's not welcomed here."

"Did Maria still have contact with him?" Molly asked.

She shook her head adamantly. "Not at all. She knows she would be in trouble." She paused and winced at her choice of words. "She *knew* how I felt about gangs and drugs. She was a great girl. The leader of her class. She was the one who stopped the fights on the playground. She was always organizing the students to do charity things like bring pennies to school to help the homeless. Imagine that! The girl had hardly nothing herself, but she never thought she was poor."

"That's because of you," Molly said. "You gave her love and that's all she needed."

Mrs. Perez processed the comment, squared her jaw and faced her. Molly saw the fierce determination in her eyes. They were the eyes Maria had inherited.

"I want you to find her killer. Promise me you'll do that."

"We'll do our best," Molly assured her.

They returned to the playground and noticed the crime scene tape had been ripped apart. Molly gazed at the bloodstain on the ground and thought she might throw up. She craved a scotch so much that she could taste it in her mouth.

Andre flipped open the file and his notebook. "Well, from what Mom added we know she left home in the late morning. Her best friend Selena Diaz, who was supposed to meet her here, never left her house, so it's likely Maria was playing alone. According to the coroner she was killed between eleven and one but I'm guessing it was before noon."

"Why do you think that?" Molly quizzed, already knowing the answer but well aware that Andre continued to hone his thinking skills. The last big mistake he'd made almost cost them an investigation and Ari's life.

"Mom wanted her to go home in an hour, and I'm sure she was going to listen to Mama."

Molly shrugged her shoulders. "That little girl was willful, and I wouldn't be surprised if she ignored rules. I'm also willing to bet she still had contact with her older brother. They looked very close in that family photo."

"Possible," Andre conceded.

Molly glanced at the school, noticing that the sun was quite bright. She said nothing but started toward the building.

"Did you get the key?"

Andre chuckled. "Check this out." He withdrew an old skeleton key from his pocket.

It took a few tries before they could open the creaky door. A slant of light showered the decrepit hallway. A junkie's paradise. She pulled a flashlight from her pocket and veered left. The air was thick with dust particles swirling in front of her face as they caught the sunlight. From above they heard a noise—the quick movement of feet. Andre withdrew his gun and flew back down the hallway, passing the entry and flying up the stairs. She stayed on his heels, their loafers pounding the ancient linoleum.

At the top of the steps they looked left and right but saw no one. Suddenly the clank of metal echoed from the first story. She darted into a classroom and stared out the window. A figure in an Army jacket, jeans and a black baseball cap bolted across the field and through the hole in the fence.

"Can't even tell if it's a man or a woman," Andre said.

"Nope," she agreed. "But we know that people spend time here during the day. It's very possible someone, maybe even that person, saw something."

"Or *did* something," he added. "I can't imagine anyone coming after that little girl intentionally. Who'd want to kill a kid?"

She shook her head and they headed toward the west corner of the building.

"Are we gonna search all of these rooms?" Andre asked, and Molly could already hear the whine in his voice again.

"No," she said, gesturing to the doors that faced the playground. "Just these. The first floor windows are too low."

They surveyed the five rooms, automatically eliminating the last two where the floor was rotted out. They were uninhabitable unless someone wanted a quick exit to the first floor. They found nothing in the next two rooms and she began to worry they wouldn't find a clue.

The end room was the biggest and contained the most trash. She peered through the dirty windows. "This is the best view of the swing set. If anyone saw anything, or if the killer was watching, he was doing it from this window."

"How do you know it was a man? Aren't you being a little chauvinistic?"

Molly scowled. "Do you really want me to cite the statistics on female killers to you?"

Andre waved his hand. "Only if you do it after we leave."

They stepped carefully, avoiding the trash and broken glass that littered the floor. A shabby mattress lay in the corner, the cracks of the hardwood planks littered with hundreds of hypodermic needles. She pulled on a pair of heavy gloves and paced the room, sometimes carefully picking up pieces of debris for examination or pushing them aside with an old yardstick she found in the corner.

Andre remained by the door trying to stay out of the way, clearly hesitant to soil his expensive suit. "Why do we care what they eat?" he complained when she emptied an old McDonald's bag.

"It's not what they eat that matters," she replied, ignoring his impatience. She'd vowed not to let him get on her nerves, but sometimes it was all she could do not to turn around and bark at him. She knew he hated dirty places because he always wore tailored suits. Ironically he had no problem tackling a suspect in his good clothes even if it meant a rip in his expensive pants, but standing in a dusty room made him nervous.

Eventually she wound up underneath the window where she meticulously sorted the trash, spreading it out, separating all of the wrappers from each other. Amid the mess she found what she was looking for.

"Check it out," she said with a smile. "I think we just got really lucky."

He stared at the white strip of paper in her hand, a receipt from the Jack in the Box down the street. The customer had purchased three plain hamburgers and a chocolate shake. It took him a second to realize why she cared—the date and the time of the purchase. Someone had purchased the food on Sunday at ten-thirty, not long before Maria Perez arrived at the playground.

"So the killer buys the food and comes here to eat it, probably getting his jollies watching Maria the whole time. Then he goes down and kills her."

"Hmm. Possibly," she said hesitantly. "And if he's not the killer then he's most likely a witness."

CHAPTER EIGHT

After ten minutes of debating whether or not they should comb the side streets of the Roosevelt neighborhood in search of the figure in the Army jacket, Molly and Andre decided to spend their time pursuing more tangible leads. They stopped by the Jack in the Box but were told the teenager who took the order had the day off. She scribbled the employee's home address in her notebook, unwilling to wait for any leads to break on the case. A quick drive to the boy's house proved fruitless since he wasn't home. Andre agreed to come back later.

Maria's school seemed the next logical stop. It was quiet as they pulled up to Phoenix Elementary Number One. The name was self-explanatory. They were sitting in front of the oldest grade school in the city. Although it had undergone at least a dozen restorations and remodeling jobs during its 160 years of existence, the framework of the original structure remained intact, with tall stone pillars rising from the foundation, sentinels for the modernized steel double doors that served as the school's front entrance. The chiseled name emblazoned across the stone front left no doubt about the importance of the edifice to the community, a symbol of the stature of education at a different time in history.

All of the children were in classes and the central corridor was empty. They found the office, which was bustling with late students and irate parents waiting to speak with an administrator. Once they flashed their badges they were quickly escorted to the conference room. The appearance of police officers superseded other business and the school principal appeared.

"Hello, I'm Cynthia Preston," she said, holding out her hand for what Molly imagined was the customary greeting that she bestowed on a multitude of people each day.

Molly met the firm handshake and was immediately impressed by Principal Preston, whose face was earnest. "I'm Detective Nelson and this is Detective Williams. We need to speak with you about Maria Perez."

Ms. Preston shook her head. She motioned for them to sit and took the chair at the head of the table. "Such a horrible tragedy. You have no idea how much this has affected our school today. The TV trucks left right before you came. All those media mongers trying to interview our parents, watching the children crying. It was ridiculous." She started to say something else and closed her mouth. She folded her hands on the table, a gesture of restraint.

Molly guessed the principal to be in her late fifties, a handsome African-American woman with a fine figure. Her makeup was meticulous yet her eyes betrayed her fatigue—and it wasn't even noon.

"Tell us about Maria," Molly said.

Ms. Preston laughed slightly as a tear rolled down her cheek. "She was one of those students who teachers loved, but it wasn't always easy. Maria challenged everyone, and she expected good answers to her questions. You earned respect from her, but once you had it, well, that child would do anything for you then." She reached for a tissue and dabbed at her eyes.

"So she was very strong willed," Andre concluded.

She nodded in agreement then added, "Not in a bad way. Maria expected fairness and justice. Although she was only a fifth-grader, she understood that a decision could be just even if she didn't agree with it."

"Did anyone at the school have a problem with her?" Molly asked.

"Well, it seems she and her friend Selena observed one of our toughest fifth-grade boys attempting to extort lunch money from a second grader."

"What did she do about it?" Molly probed, already fearing the answer.

"Just what you would expect. She confronted the boy and got in his face. A teacher saw them arguing and came over to intervene. We have these kinds of problems all the time, but the reason I mention it is because the bully was Raul Cervantes, brother of Hector Cervantes. And I'm assuming you know that Maria was Franco Perez's younger sister."

Molly scribbled several notes furiously. "So you're concerned because you think it's possible that Hector may have killed her because she tattled?"

"Detective, you need to understand something about Hector Cervantes and Franco Perez. Everything you read in the news about these young men is true. They epitomize what all the songs and movies exploit about gang members. They have killed people over nothing, and they will look for any opportunity to express their hatred. Would it surprise me if this whole incident is about the problem between Maria and Raul? Not at all. And Hector Cervantes is an extremely stubborn man. His mother is dead, and his father abandoned him and his brother when they were young. Hector *is* Raul's father and there's no way he would ever let anyone disrespect Raul. He was suspended over the incident and Hector knows that he's very close to being expelled from the school district. I don't know if that's enough reason for Hector to kill Maria, but I can assure you that there was certainly some type of retaliation that occurred. There always is."

"We need to interview Maria's friend Selena Diaz as well as Raul Cervantes," Molly said.

Ms. Preston nodded. Her secretary stuck her head into the room and she excused herself.

"So, what do you make of this?" Andre asked. "Do you really think a gang-banger would take out a little girl over a suspension?"

Molly rubbed her chin and stared at her notes. She guessed that Maria loved to stir up trouble. She seemed fearless, a necessary South Phoenix survival trait but one that could have been her undoing. She pictured her standing up to Raul Cervantes, those brown eyes blazing, ignoring the consequences. Could it have earned her a bullet in the chest? A wave of admiration and fear simultaneously touched her heart.

The conference room door squeaked open again and the principal's secretary returned. "I'm sorry. Ms. Preston needs to meet with the superintendent. I'm Mrs. Jones and I've called Raul down, but Selena isn't in school today. I've left a message with Hector. I'm sure he'll be here quickly. If you'll follow me, I'll take you to a quieter area."

They followed Mrs. Jones through the busy hallways filled with students changing classes. As they passed the rows of lockers, a huge banner hanging from the staircase caught Molly's attention. The large red letters advertised a city-wide science fair and congratulated Mrs. Stimson's fifth-grade class for placing first in the competition.

Molly gazed skyward and Mrs. Jones pointed at the banner. "That was Maria's class. They're an awesome group and totally devastated by her death. It's such a shame. They just won last week, and we were going to honor them tomorrow. Now I don't think anyone wants to celebrate."

Mrs. Jones ushered them into the library and retrieved Raul. Molly was surprised when a scrawny, short boy with a buzz cut stepped into the room. Wearing a simple white T-shirt that drooped well below his saggy shorts, she concluded that he couldn't carry the gangster image he was trying to convey.

"Raul, this is Detective Nelson and she needs to ask you some questions."

"I want my brother here," he said, his gaze avoiding Molly.

"He's on his way."

She motioned to a small table and whispered in Molly's ear. "I'm sure Hector will be here in a few minutes. He doesn't work that far away. If you want any information, you'd better get it quick. When he gets here, he won't let him talk."

She nodded in appreciation and sat down next to him.

"I'll go wait for your brother in the office, Raul," Mrs. Jones said before she left.

Molly watched him, his teeth nervously biting into his lower lip as his left leg bopped up and down. He stared at a shelf of books, reading the spines. She let the silence settle between them, resisting the urge to shotgun a series of questions at him before Hector interrupted the session.

"Have you read any of those books?" she asked. He nodded, totally disinterested in the small talk. Still she pressed on, determined to find a point of interest that might hook him. "Which ones?"

"Just *The Outsiders*," he mumbled.

A book about a gang of boys. Not surprising. She'd read the classic years ago, but she couldn't remember much about it. There were themes about loyalty, friendship and family, all of which she was sure he could relate to.

"Who was your favorite character?"

"Ponyboy."

"Why?"

He shrugged. "I don't know. I just remember that I liked him."

"That's cool," she said, before a long pause. "Raul, I've got a murder to investigate, and I need your help."

"I want my brother," he said plainly.

"Just chill, kid. You're not in any trouble," Andre snapped.

She realized how smart he was, and she wouldn't be able to blow over him like she could with most other children she interviewed. "It would help me if you'd just tell me what you know about Maria Perez."

"She's a snitch," he blurted. "She got me in trouble."

He immediately closed his mouth, realizing his brother wouldn't approve. She could tell he was struggling to control his anger. His knee jerked faster. He wouldn't look at her.

"Was it really Maria who got you in trouble or did you do it to yourself?"

She posed the question exactly as her older brother did with his own children. His response, though, was much different than that of her niece and nephew. Instead of looking remotely penitent he glared at her. He had his version of the truth, and he wouldn't be manipulated by child psychology.

"You don't understand anything," he said. "Maria was a fake. She wasn't all perfect, and she was a liar. She just wanted everyone else to get in trouble while she got away with stuff."

"Like what?" Molly asked.

He shook his head, and his gaze fell to the floor. "I'm not gonna say. I'm not a snitch. I'm not her."

She watched him closely, his lip quivering. She understood the code of ethics that surrounded most middle school boys. He was nervous, but there was no way he would give anyone up to an adult. "What did your brother think of her?"

"Hector?" He looked surprised. "Hector didn't care about her."

"Hector didn't care that she got you suspended, almost kicked out of school?"

"No, I didn't care," said a voice from the doorway. Hector Cervantes swaggered beside his younger brother, placing a protective hand on his shoulder. "Didn't I tell you to always wait for me?"

"I told her, but she kept asking me questions," he whined.

He whispered something in Spanish to his brother. Raul nodded and quickly left the room, not bothering to look at her again while Hector lowered himself into the chair his brother had vacated.

"If you want to talk to me, then talk to *me*. Raul knows nothing to help you."

Molly held his gaze, well aware that to look away or even blink would be a sign of weakness in the presence of an alleged killer. Perhaps Hector didn't kill Maria, but the brown eyes that bored into hers were hardened, darkened by the knowledge of death.

"Mr. Cervantes, I'm Detective Nelson and this is Detective Williams. Okay, I'll ask you. What do you know about Maria Perez's murder?"

He folded his arms, elaborate gang tattoos peeking out from under his mechanic's work shirt. He was much more muscular than Raul and Molly guessed—no fighter would ever get the best of him. His slicked back hair and sculpted Van Dyke only added to the tough image and the typical look of a warlord.

"I know she took one in the chest at the drugstore."

"The drugstore? Is that Washington School?"

The corners of his mouth lifted into a slight smile. "Ain't no schoolin' going on there anymore. Just lots of buys."

Her anger surfaced as she pictured a giant wrecking ball crashing into the structure. Nothing good would ever come of that place again.

"Is that where you deal?"

He laughed. "Detective, I am a law-abiding citizen."

"So you don't know anything about this little girl's murder?" Andre asked impatiently.

He tapped his fingers against his workpants, ignoring the question. It was clear he wasn't afraid of their badges in the least. He propped his feet up on a nearby chair and stretched back. "I'm not saying anything to you. You know nothing about what goes on down here."

"So educate us. Tell us why anyone would want to kill a ten-year-old girl in cold blood?"

He snorted and shook his head. "It happens all the time, lady."

She leaned closer. "Well, you obviously knew about her murder or you did it yourself."

He scowled and sat up in the chair. "Why do cops always assume that Latino men are responsible for crime if it occurs in the barrio?"

"Because they usually are," she shot back.

He stood and headed for the door. "Maria Perez was a troublemaker, and I'm not surprised she got popped."

"So can I assume Raul didn't like her?" she called.

He let out a sound of disapproval. "Detective, if I were you, I'd stay away from Raul." His voice was cold and soft and she felt a shiver down her back.

"Are you threatening me?"

He grinned slightly. "Of course not, Detective. Like I said, I'm a law-abiding citizen."

He walked out of the room, his relaxed saunter mocking her.

CHAPTER NINE

It was late afternoon by the time Ari returned to her office after previewing several houses in North Scottsdale for Stan Wertz. She immediately headed for the refrigerator, hoping to find two of Lorraine's famous tamales for lunch. Dinner with her father and Sol wasn't scheduled until eight, and she imagined her stomach would be growling fiercely.

She wolfed down the tamales and powered up her computer, attempting to learn more about her new client. She downloaded several articles from a Google search and learned Wertz had spent his entire life in the grocery business. He'd risen from the bottom of the ladder, beginning as a bag boy at the first Hometown Grocery. When he finally broke into management and purchased the small company, he saw the possibility of expansion and bought land for a second store. A second led to a third and eventually there were Hometown Groceries all over Phoenix.

She scrolled through a story detailing how he'd forced a family restaurant out of the location it had enjoyed for twenty years to acquire the land for one of his stores. Despite the pleas of the communi, and even some nasty editorials in *The Arizona Republic*, he'd had the sheriff's office escort the patriarch off the property, drawing negative publicity and picketers on the sidewalks outside the other stores.

His mettle continued to be tested by the presence of FoodCo, the mega-conglomerate that gobbled up all of the other grocery chains. There were now only two food companies in Phoenix: FoodCo, whose storefronts bore many names, and Hometown Grocery. He refused to sell to FoodCo despite numerous offers.

The final article was only three days old and announced an opening of another Hometown Grocery in Gilbert. She scrolled through the particulars but found no connection to Warren Edgington. In the article Wertz boasted that he had every intention of keeping his foothold in the Phoenix grocery competition and his bigger plans included a store that could rival any big box store.

She leaned back in her chair and tented her fingers under her chin, thinking about what she had learned about him. He was obviously powerful and ruthless, not afraid to achieve his goals at the expense of others. She wasn't surprised that he'd confronted Edgington in public. But what were they talking about?

She typed in Edgington's name and found his website. He was a commercial real estate investor and speculator. After she clicked on all the links she'd still learned very little. He'd created a teaser, a website designed to give prospective clients a preview but not much real information. Anyone interested in Mr. Edgington's services would need to call. When she scrolled to the bottom she found a message from his wife, thanking his clients for their past business and notes of condolence.

She closed the articles and began writing her thoughts into the file. A knock drew her eyes to the doorway. A slash of dark hair leaned casually against the jamb, her thumbs looped into the front pockets of her jeans. The visitor smiled broadly at Ari.

Ari swallowed hard at the sight of Biz Stone, a private investigator who'd helped save Jane's life recently. "Hello, Biz," she said.

"Hey." Biz motioned behind her. "There wasn't anybody in the lobby so I came on through. I hope I didn't scare you."

"No, of course not. I'm sorry there wasn't anyone to greet you. Our receptionist leaves at four."

Biz shrugged, bypassing the client chairs and strolling to the couch with a sense of familiarity. She sat down and stretched her legs. Ari noticed that today she wore a Joan Jett and the Blackhearts T-shirt with her tight jeans. She looked incredibly sexy. *That's why you need to stay away from her.*

"It's been a while, Biz."

Biz glanced at her watch. "Three months, nineteen days and nine hours."

She smiled weakly. "You're very precise. What are you doing here?"

Biz sat up and rested her hands on her knees. "Actually I'm here on business. I'm looking for a real estate agent. I want to buy a place."

She shifted in her seat while warning bells went off in her head. She knew if she joined Biz on the couch and stared into her brown eyes with the gold flecks, she would become confused again, lost in dangerous feelings. That couldn't happen. She raised her head with complete resolve. "I can't help you, Biz. You know that. You need to ask Lorraine."

Biz held up her hands. "Why do I need Lorraine? I thought we were friends."

"We are friends, but you know as well as I do that our relationship is complicated."

"Complicated? Complicated by what?"

Ari glared and Biz feigned recognition. "Oh, you mean Molly. It's complicated because she has a problem with me being in your life and you don't want to upset her—"

"No, that's not it at all. You've summarized everything incorrectly. Molly doesn't have a problem—"

"So, you do?"

She sighed in exasperation. "No, I don't have a problem."

Biz jumped up and started pacing. "Well, I don't have a problem. Maybe it's Jane. Maybe she has the problem or maybe it's the waiter at Oregano's. Maybe he has the problem."

"Stop," she said.

She looked at Biz, totally dejected. She couldn't explain her feelings. She knew helping her was wrong. It was a risk that would jeopardize her relationship with Molly. It was irrational, but it was the truth.

"I can't," she said simply.

Biz strolled behind her chair and hovered over her. She said nothing for a long time, allowing their nearness to wash over her.

"I don't want to ask Lorraine or Jane," she whispered. "If we're truly friends then this shouldn't be a problem. And if your relationship with Molly can't endure a *business* client, who also happens to be attracted to you, then it'll never last with her."

She returned to the other side of the desk and dropped into a client chair. "Besides I'm going to make you a ton of money."

The money is the last thing I care about.

But Biz was right. What would happen the first time an attractive lesbian client hit on her? Was Molly going to be jealous of every single woman in her life? This shouldn't be an issue. She'd just have to figure out a way to tell Molly.

Ari looked into her incredible eyes. "Okay, here are the ground rules. No flirting. No touching. No passes. Strictly professional. Does that work for you?"

She grinned. "Not really, but I'll work it out in therapy."

Ari suppressed a smile and picked up a pen. "Fine. Tell me what you're looking for."

She took a deep breath, as if she was preparing to make a speech. "I'm not sure what I want but I'm sick of renting. I want to own something. That whole American dream crap." She leaned forward on the desk. "Don't you ever want that?"

She shrugged. "Sometimes. But for now I rent."

"Alone?"

Suddenly she felt uncomfortable. She knew Biz was only half joking and the comment unnerved her. "For now," she replied simply. "So what do you picture when you see yourself sitting at home?"

Biz stared out the window. Her unruly hair dropped back over her eyes, adding to her sexiness. "Well, I want many things, but I guess I'm looking for a loft, something that reminds me of New York. Maybe downtown. I know I don't want anything remotely close to suburbia. I can't stand the cookie-cutter look."

"Me either," she agreed. "So you want something urban. What about a converted industrial place?"

Biz's face brightened. "That would be great. With lots of windows and open space. Do you know anything like that?"

"Yes, there's a new development near Chase Field. It was a factory and they remodeled each floor into four separate lofts. I've seen the website and it looks fantastic."

"That sounds perfect. Can you show me?"

"Sure. I'll pull it up for you."

She clicked through a series of screens while Biz pulled her chair around next to her. "It's called Trombetta Dwellings and it's a relatively new developer who wants to come in and save the inner cities. It's got a ton of amenities including a fitness center and a spa. And they're opening retail shops down in the lobby for the residents. Places like a dry cleaners and a pharmacy."

"That would be so convenient," Biz murmured as she studied the plans. "I hate to shop." Ari giggled and they faced each other.

"What?" Biz laughed.

She shook her head and gazed into the brown eyes—but only for a second. She felt heat flow through her body. "I hate shopping too. I'd have everything delivered if I could."

"Errands," Biz whispered. Ari felt her breath float across the top of her ear. "The enemy of Saturday morning." They both chuckled while Ari clicked through the pages of the website. When the interiors appeared on the screen, Biz leaned forward and studied the layout. "This looks great. When can I see it?"

"I could call them tomorrow morning and make an appointment, but they're very expensive."

She grinned. "What? You don't think I can afford it? Make the appointment."

"When are you available?"

"Any time. Let me know."

She was staring into her eyes, lost. When Biz moved closer, Ari jumped. "I'll set up the appointment as soon as possible and call you. And I'm sorry if I sounded like I was judging you," she added, as she walked her out to her car, a '67 Shelby 350.

"Don't worry about it," Biz said. "I consider it a plus that in my profession I get to wear my entire collection of concert T-shirts. The downside is that people usually think I'm homeless and unemployed."

She laughed. "I wish I had that freedom."

Biz's eyes wandered up and down her body. "And so, Ms. Adams, what would you choose to wear if you weren't shackled by the fashion sense of the rich snobs who judge your clothes the first time they meet you?"

"I don't know. Something casual."

Biz touched her arm. "I'll bet you'd look fantastic in a pair of tight leather pants and a tank top. It would go great with your new motorcycle."

She rolled her eyes at the mention of her father's recent birthday present. "I don't think so," she said.

"Have you ridden it yet?"

She shook her head, conscious that Biz still held her arm.

"My offer still stands. I'd be glad to teach you how to ride."

"I don't think so. I'll probably just sell it when I have time."

"That would be a terrible waste." She tipped Ari's chin until they gazed into each other's eyes. "I want you to make me a promise."

"What?" she whispered.

Biz's finger stroked the side of her cheek, and her knees went weak. "I want you to promise me that before you sell that incredible machine you'll at least let me take you out on it. You need to know what you're missing."

She closed her eyes momentarily, oblivious to Biz's words. When she finally opened them, Biz was grinning. *She knows she has power over me.*

With that thought she burst the bubble Biz had wrapped her in and scowled. "You've broken every rule we agreed to. You've flirted. You've touched me, and you've clearly made a pass at me."

Biz shook her head in disagreement. "I haven't made a pass at you, at least nothing really overt."

"And what would you call that last move?"

Biz hooked her finger inside Ari's waistband. "That was just testing the waters. Do you really want to know how I make a pass at a woman, an incontrovertible and obvious pass?"

She remained motionless, unable to move or speak. Biz was too close and the sexual energy between them was debilitating. She just stood there, praying Biz would leave soon, before Lorraine came out or Molly drove up. Of course if Molly pulled up right at that moment, they would make the newspapers, for she'd pull her gun out and kill Biz.

But Biz just continued to smile, her finger stroking Ari's belly. "If I were really going to make a pass, I'd kiss you. I'd kiss you hard. I'd kiss you so deeply that I'd pull all the breath out of you."

Biz's comment rang in her ears, and she was too stunned to respond. Common sense pulled her away, and she retreated inside the office. She leaned against the wall for support. She remained there, breathing deeply until the sound of the Shelby's engine roared out of the neighborhood.

CHAPTER TEN

The woman called Checkers clucked her tongue four, five, six times—a nervous tick she could no longer control. It was an inevitable holdover from her days as a smoker, a habit she hadn't been able to afford for years.

Seven. Eight. Nine.

The Greyhound bus terminal was busy since it was a Monday, and the security guards wouldn't notice her for a while. She slipped into a molded plastic chair in the bustling lobby and glanced up at the TV in the corner. Her favorite show *Law and Order* was playing, featuring Briscoe and Green. She loved Lennie Briscoe. He reminded her of Sully with his thick New York accent and his "tell it like it is" attitude.

She missed Sully, but that was a lifetime ago back when she had a home.

And Laurie. Her dear, sweet Laurie.

Tears welled in her eyes, and she sniffed. No point in thinking about the old days. They were over and would never return. Sully was dead and Laurie was gone. Briscoe and Green stood over a body, a crimson stain at the base of his skull. She shuddered involuntarily at the sight. So much violence, so much blood. Or had she imagined it?

It hadn't seemed real. Her dear friend Professor Shakespeare had bought her a hamburger, and she'd taken it back to the old schoolhouse and eaten it in the empty classroom that faced the swingset. No one was there to bother her, and she loved watching the children play.

Ten, eleven, twelve.

Pictures scrolled through her mind like the old-time movies at the Coney Island arcade. She'd pay her penny and crank the handle, watching the sepia images flip over one on top of the other, faster and faster.

Like the swinging. The little girl going higher and higher, a smile on her face. Just like her Laurie. Laurie loved the swings.

She'd seen the dark man coming before the little girl. He looked wrong. He wasn't supposed to be there. She couldn't call out to her! It was like watching TV. There was nothing she could do to help Briscoe and Green.

Then he stood in front of her, the gun in his hand. She had tapped on the window and cried out—too late!

The little girl on the dirt, a halo of red over her heart, like the one Briscoe and Green saw. There was more, but the images were turning. Too fast! She couldn't stop to see. And the blood on her hands. How did the blood get there?

"Checkers, what are you doing here?" a baritone voice asked.

She grinned and met his stare. "Just hangin', Bruce."

He laughed. "Aw, Checkers. You know I can't let you stay here. Rules are rules even if you remind me of my grandmother."

She continued to smile at the tall, thin black man who couldn't be more than twenty-five. He barely filled out his uniform, and the sight of him reminded her of the first time she'd seen Sully in his military dress blues. She'd fallen in love with him at that very moment.

"C'mon, Checkers. I'll buy you a Coke."

Bribery always worked. She pulled herself up, grateful to get something out of the deal. That was life on the streets. If it didn't work for you, it wasn't your friend.

She walked with him to the concessions stand, checking her pocket for the five dollar bill that a kind, well-dressed lady had slipped her that morning.

Thirteen. Fourteen. Fifteen.

Still, there was something important to remember, but she couldn't think of it. The pictures. The blood.

Bruce handed her the cup of promised refreshment, and she shuffled to the doorway, her eyes glancing up at the TV screen over the bar. She stopped, almost dropping her drink in the process. A woman sat at a news desk, a stack of papers in her hand, her serious expression recounting the details of a tragic accident on the Beeline Highway. Checkers couldn't believe what she was seeing. Bold white script bannered the bottom of the picture, announcing the woman as Laurel Ann Jeffries.

Her Laurie.

CHAPTER ELEVEN

Molly popped two aspirin, glanced at the third one that had fallen into her hand and downed it as well. She rubbed her temples and stared at the Perez file. The interview with Hector Cervantes had left her cold. It was clear that the only person he cared for besides himself was his brother. If Hector felt Maria Perez was a threat to Raul, Molly knew she would've paid.

"Nelson," a voice called from the doorway.

She closed her eyes for an instant, wishing Captain David Ruskin would vanish, but when she looked up he'd entered her office, his jacket thrown over his shoulder, obviously leaving for the day.

"Where are we with Perez?"

His voice sounded accusatory, as if the killer should be caught by now. "We've got some leads. It's looking like it might be gang related."

He rolled his eyes. "Since when do gangs take out kids?"

She knew there was no point in explaining the investigation to him. He really had no interest in the facts and would never engage in any type of information exchange with her. "It's just a possibility," she said.

"We need more than that, Nelson. We need results. You and Williams ought to be able to handle *one* major investigation now that Edgington's file is closed. It's not like you've got a lot more on your plate, right?"

"Give her a break, Dave."

She shifted her gaze to the large figure in the doorway, a man the size of a bear—Big Jack Adams. She swallowed hard and wished she could crawl under her desk.

Ruskin said nothing as he shuffled his feet. Adams moved very close and dwarfed him.

"I can't imagine you've been out in the field within the last decade. I doubt you know how hard Detective Nelson is working."

Molly bit her lip, trying not to laugh.

Ruskin's whole face moved but he said nothing. Without ever acknowledging Jack, he barked, "I want something concrete by tomorrow," before he stomped out.

Jack waved good-bye and chuckled. "I'm Jack Adams, and you're Molly Nelson."

She nodded and met his strong handshake. "Great to meet you. Thanks for all of your help with the John Rondo investigation," she said, referring to a case he'd helped her with a few months before.

He crammed his large body into the visitor's chair. "I should thank you. I guess I miss being in the game. Retirement hasn't been an easy adjustment."

"I can only imagine. I don't know what I'd do if I wasn't a cop."

He met her gaze and nodded. She felt a kinship with him, and when she looked at his face, she saw traces of Ari. Her cell phone rang with Ari's ringtone, the old Safaris' song *Wipeout.*

"Um, excuse me, but I have to take this."

She jumped out of the chair and went to the hallway. "Hey."

"Hi, baby. How was your day?"

"Great." She glanced toward her office. Jack was studying her two framed commendations. "Aren't you going to dinner with your dad?"

"Yeah, but that's not until eight. I'm taking him out for Greek. If nothing else it'll be entertaining and give us a few conversation starters."

"It can't be that bad, can it? I've heard he's a great guy."

Ari sighed. "It's just hard, babe. There's a lot of history, you know? He threw me out, remember? Disowned his gay daughter?"

"Of course, honey. I understand. Forget what I said. This case really has me bummed. We had to go to the coroner's today and watch the autopsy. I can't tell you how hard it was."

"Honey, I'm sorry. You would've been better off with the Edgington case."

"Well, I'm gonna get whoever did this. The mother's totally distraught and confused. It's not like the girl had any enemies." Hector Cervantes's smug grin flashed in her memory—she quickly thought better than to worry Ari about the details of their encounter. "We have a few leads. Someone, maybe the killer, was watching from a room inside the school. I hate that damn school," she added absently. "The whole place should be leveled to get rid of all the dealers and junkies."

"But that's an historic building," Ari argued. "I mean it's horrible what happened to that little girl, but that's not the school's fault. The city should do a better job keeping people out of there."

"You mean the police," she clarified. She couldn't believe what she was hearing.

"Well, maybe there should be more police presence," Ari said slowly.

"I see. It would be better for the cops to be out patrolling vacant, abandoned buildings, which by the way are unsafe for humans to inhabit, rather than following up on rapes and murders. That makes sense."

"That's not what I mean, honey. C'mon, I'm not even thinking about what I'm saying here. I'm getting ready for an evening with my father. Cut me some slack, please?"

She felt her anger sliding away, but instead of letting go, instead of turning toward the warmth and friendliness of her voice, she pulled the confrontation back between them.

She glanced back to her office. Jack was checking his voice mail on his BlackBerry. "So are you finally going to tell your father about us tonight?" she asked with resentment.

"Maybe. I'm not sure. I want to tell him about you, but we need to talk about other stuff first. There's so much in our past—"

"What about the *present*? Isn't that what's most important? Am I important?"

"Of course you're important. You just don't understand."

She could hear the frustration in Ari's voice, but she was tired of being the invisible girlfriend. "I guess I don't. I thought when you said *I love you* it meant something."

"Of course it means something," Ari replied, her voice cracking.

"Well, I'm not so sure."

When Ari was silent and offered no further protests, she felt her anxieties wrap around her gut. She opened her mouth, knowing she'd gone too far.

"I'm rather sorry I called," Ari said icily, cutting off her chance for an apology. "This is obviously not a good time. Maybe we could talk tomorrow."

She closed her eyes in defeat, understanding the double message. Ari was hurt, and she didn't want them to spend the night together.

"Fine," she whispered.

She snapped her cell phone shut and shook her head. Why did she pick a fight?

She returned to her office just as Jack was standing to go. "I'm sorry that took so long."

He waved his hand. "Don't worry about it. I remember those days. I need to get going anyway. I'm meeting my daughter for dinner. Maybe we could grab a drink at Oaxaca sometime," he suggested, referring to the nearby cop watering hole.

"That would be great," she said brightly. If Ari ever managed to reveal their relationship to Jack, she imagined the three of them could share some laughs.

He left and her eyes drifted to her messy desk and the day's newspaper that lay in front of her. Ironically she was connected with both of the top stories—the murder of Maria Perez and the suicide of Warren Edgington. She'd gained one case and lost the other. She grabbed Edgington's autopsy report and scanned it. Traces of pills and alcohol had been found in his system. His wife had admitted that she was thinking of divorce after discovering he'd had an affair with a mystery woman that the police couldn't seem to locate.

She frowned. She hated loose ends, but people caught up in affairs took many steps to hide their identities. *Still, there was that key with the red and white twist-ties. A key to the lover's house or apartment?* Probably a dead end. Yet Ari wasn't totally convinced it was suicide. She rubbed her temples. She needed to let it go.

She picked up the newspaper again and gazed at a picture of Edgington with his family on their yacht, smiling and content, obviously all a sham.

The wealth and luxuriousness of the Edgingtons' lives contrasted to the simple school photo of Maria Perez just a few columns away on the front page. Such vastly different existences. It was clear the newspaper preferred writing about the tragedy of a depressed businessman who had everything to lose rather than the death of a little Hispanic girl whose family had gang ties.

She sighed in disgust and pulled out the spreadsheet of addresses. Somewhere among all the numbers was a key to a department mole, someone who was a leak and working for a crime family. She studied Andre's notes, realizing that many of the upscale addresses were owned by corporations. These probably warranted more scrutiny.

Andre knocked on the door ten minutes later, interrupting her progress. The look on his face told her something was wrong.

"What?" Molly asked.

"I went back to Selena Diaz's house to ask about the science fair, but she wasn't there."

Molly shrugged her shoulders. "So she wasn't home. You'll go back tomorrow."

"No, Mol. That's not what I mean. They're *gone*. The whole family's left."

CHAPTER TWELVE

When Ari spilled her morning coffee all over a contract after she'd stubbed her toe on the credenza, she looked longingly at her bed. The Egyptian sheets and feather pillows called to her, tempting her to give up on the day and crawl back under the covers. She could easily rationalize that she should heed these omens. Instead she carefully cleaned up the mess, calculating that re-writing the contract would consume an extra hour from somewhere in her day.

She realized she was in a foul mood because of the fight with Molly. She had slept alone on a night they traditionally shared, and it was her own doing. She'd been angry and wanted to punish her. She'd punished herself as well. But Molly had said some cruel things to her, and although she'd come very close to mentioning their relationship at dinner with her father, she'd side-stepped the issue.

She thought about the initial awkwardness of the evening

with him, which was why she had chosen Bacchanal, a Greek restaurant with belly dancers and performers. Discussing the finer points of belly dancing had definitely broken the ice and given them plenty of conversation openings.

After several rounds of Ouzo, he'd asked loudly, "Who's the love of your life?"

"I'm not going to discuss it," she said.

She'd glanced over at Sol, her godfather and Molly's highest-ranking boss, who watched the exchange between them.

Jack leaned closer. "I'm not asking for details, honey. I just want to know that you're happy."

"Of course she's happy," Sol interjected, slapping Jack on the back. "Why wouldn't she be? She's young, gorgeous and incredible at her job." He raised his glass in salute. "Ari, darling, if I'd had any daughters, I hope they all would've been just like you."

She blushed. Sol had fathered three boys, all of whom were highly successful. In fact before Ari had come out, Sol and Jack had regularly tried to set her up with Sol's youngest son.

"Look," Jack pressed, "I just know that it sucks being alone. It's important to find someone. That's all."

She was touched by his sentiment, and the words nearly fell from her lips, but a belly dancer twirled to their table and pulled Jack away to dance. She wasn't surprised when the woman wrapped her arms around his neck and thrust her chest in his face. All women were charmed by Jack Adams, but she'd never seen him flirt with anyone except her mother.

"I understand why you're waiting to tell him, Ari. I think you're doing the right thing," Sol said while Jack danced. "You need to do this in your own way."

She smiled weakly. "Thanks for understanding, Sol. I wish Molly could."

"Are you guys okay?" he asked.

She nodded. "Yeah, but she's really upset about her case. She hates it when kids are the victims."

"Don't we all," he said.

They both watched Jack shake and shimmy with the dancer. At one point she pushed him onto a floor cushion, removed his shoes and tied his socks together. When he stood to dance, the crowd roared and clapped.

Overall she thought the night was a success as she pulled into the parking lot for her Tuesday morning ritual with Jane. She sighed when she saw the line snaking out the door of Java's. She was due to meet Stan Wertz in forty-five minutes. She scanned the couches and chairs and found Jane deeply engaged in conversation with a seductive brunette dressed in an expensive suit. The two of them could have been twins, their dark hair, perfect makeup and expensive jewelry separating them from the middleclass mocha latté drinkers surrounding them.

She wandered through the crowd and caught Jane's attention. The brunette turned around, and she realized she was staring at Laurel Jeffries, the new six o'clock anchor for Channel Fifteen and Jane's most needy client. Jane waved at Ari and pointed to a large coffee setting on the coffee table in front of them.

"Thank you," she said with relief, taking the cup.

"Ari, this is Laurel Jeffries."

Laurel smiled and raised her own coffee in salute. Ari joined them hesitantly, sensing she was interrupting something.

"Have you found a house yet, Laurel?"

Laurel beamed at Jane and patted her knee. "Jane says she has the perfect place for me. We're going there today after I do the mid-morning news."

"Great," Ari said.

"Where's Molly?" Jane asked.

Her cheeks reddened as she sipped her coffee. "She couldn't come. She's busy with her big case."

"What case is that?" Laurel asked with her journalistic curiosity.

"She's working the Maria Perez murder." She figured that much would be common knowledge soon.

"Do they have any leads?" Laurel pressed. "I mean it's just so horrible."

She shrugged knowing that to say anymore would guarantee she spent the rest of her nights without Molly in her bed.

Laurel checked her watch and stood. "Well, I have to go. Ari, it was a pleasure, and Jane, I'll see you in a few hours." Laurel blew Jane a kiss and departed with her latté in hand.

Ari noticed a little grin spreading across Jane's face as she watched Laurel's perfect ass sway out the door. Jane faced her, and she chuckled.

"What?" Jane cried.

She laughed. "I take it you and the TV lady are getting along?"

"What are you suggesting? Laurel and I have a highly professional relationship. The fact that we share the same incredible taste in fashion, know all of the best wine bars in the valley and believe that post-Modern art is a travesty, doesn't mean that I want to take her to bed. That would be violating my long-standing rule about screwing clients."

She patted her knee. "Sweetie, you can't claim to have a rule if you're always breaking it."

Jane considered this while she stirred her coffee. "Then I guess it's a guideline. That allows me *some* flexibility, right?" Her eyes narrowed. "Now really, where is Molly? She's always here on Tuesday morning."

She lowered her eyes and blinked away tears. "We had a fight." She looked around the crowded room and shook her head. "I really don't want to talk about this right now, okay?"

Jane squeezed her hand with her finely manicured fingers. "Okay. But you do need to tell me about dinner with your father. How did that go?"

"It was fine. He wants to see you."

"We'll all do lunch. I'm free today."

She sighed and shook her head. "I'm not. I'm previewing houses for the slimiest man I've ever met."

Jane clapped her hands. "Okay, it's time for coffee catharsis."

She grinned at the mention of their favorite game where they discussed new clients they'd acquired or complained about the ones who drove them nuts.

"I won't even talk about Laurel today," Jane said. "I'm certain she'll love the listing I'm showing her later. What's new with you?"

"I got a new client. Biz."

Jane's perfectly shadowed eyes widened, and her blood red lips parted in amazement. "Biz Stone is your client? How did that happen?"

She shrugged. "She walked in yesterday afternoon around four. She wants to buy a loft."

Jane carefully set the coffee stirrer onto the napkin. When she looked up, her face was devoid of all humor. "And do you really think it's going to help your relationship with Molly when she finds out that you're working with Biz?"

She leaned back in the chair, unable to argue. "I can't explain it, Jane. She's very persuasive, and it's a ton of money."

"That's never been a motivation for you, Ari, and you know it. You need to be honest with yourself even if you can't be honest with me."

"I am being honest. I want to work with Biz and Molly needs to get over it. If we really have a future, she's going to have to learn to trust me." Jane didn't respond immediately, and she shifted uncomfortably in her seat. "Say something."

Jane took a deep breath and met her gaze. "That speech would be far more impressive if you trusted yourself. But you don't. And you shouldn't. Not when it comes to Biz." She squeezed her hand. "Be careful, sweetie. You're up in a very high tree and out on a shaky limb and there's not a cute firewoman in sight to catch you when you fall."

Ari's stomach flip-flopped as she pulled up to Stan Wertz's Day Arbor house, but she smiled at the inviting front yard and the shrubbery that framed the exterior. It was so pleasant and screamed curbside appeal. She noticed Lorraine's sign was already up, doubting it would take very long for an offer to arrive. She headed to the door realizing that she disliked him almost as much as she liked his home. Lorraine had sensed her hesitation to work with him, but it was clear she wanted the deal to happen for both of them.

Dora answered the door and led her into the living room when the phone rang.

"Will you excuse me for a moment?" she asked, clearly flustered that her first task was being interrupted.

"Not a problem," Ari said.

She retreated into the kitchen and when she didn't return right away, Ari wandered into the man cave. She shook her head again at the sight of the pole, but her eyes drifted toward the flasks at the top of the bar. She scanned them one by one, comparing them in her mind to the one in Edgington's car, but all of these seemed much older. She cruised through the room unsure of what she thought it would tell her.

Her eyes landed on a dartboard against the wall over the poker table. Much of the board was obscured by small slips of paper pinned to the board by darts. She looked closely, realizing they were IOUs. Each slip had a name and an amount written in different handwriting—and one of the slips read *Warren, 10K*. Quite possibly Warren Edgington owed Stan Wertz ten thousand dollars. More importantly, they were poker buddies. She wondered if Molly knew they'd shared a personal relationship.

"I'm so sorry," Dora said, appearing at the door.

She immediately mustered a quick lie, but Dora only motioned for her to follow without question. She escorted her out to the car house where she found Wertz polishing the hood of an exotic automobile that she couldn't name. The small garage was pristine and empty except for a few oak cabinets, a sink and the vehicle itself. Clearly the only reason for the building's existence was to act as a safe haven for the prized possession.

"It's a nineteen thirty-two Ford roadster convertible," he said.

She nodded, although she knew nothing about cars. She admired the tiny doors and little headlights that looked like eyes. Not her style, but she thought it was cute.

"Have you ever seen a machine as incredibly beautiful as this, Ari?"

"No," she answered, realizing that he would probably not appreciate her description. He lovingly massaged each bumper with a soft chamois. She watched silently since his attention was singularly focused on his task. She had apparently intruded on what was a religious experience for him.

Once the soft rag had touched every inch of the car, he washed his hands and opened the passenger door. "Shall we go?" he motioned in gentlemanly fashion.

"Oh, I thought we were going in my SUV."

"No, no. I want to drive. Nothing would make me happier than cruising down Scottsdale Road with a beautiful woman at my side."

She muffled her temper as she climbed in. She quickly regrouped her presentation in her mind and tried to organize her files on her lap. They pulled onto the street, and he draped his left arm over the back of the seat. Anyone observing them would think they were a couple—a wealthy older man and his young trophy wife out to be seen in Scottsdale.

He seemed to drive incredibly slow, making the trip longer than necessary. They finally headed into the neighborhood of the first house on her list, a contemporary McMansion. She entered the alarm code into the keypad, and the wrought iron gates slowly parted, allowing the roadster to meander up the long driveway to the expansive front door.

She retrieved the keys from the lockbox and opened the door for him. "Let's see," she said, reading from the listing. "This spacious home was built in two thousand two by Talaveria. It has eight bedrooms and six bathrooms, including an upper master suite with a balcony that overlooks the ninth hole of Verde Greens. A thousand square-foot guesthouse sits on the northwest side of the property." She turned to face Wertz, who was leaning against the entryway wall. "Where do you want to start?"

"What I'd really like is for you to undo the next two buttons of your blouse," he said in a matter-of-fact tone.

She looked up, stunned. "Excuse me?"

He shifted his feet, his hands deep in his pockets and a schoolboy grin on his face. "It's very difficult to look down your shirt with all those buttons fastened. And I've certainly tried all the way over here. A few more buttons would make me a happy man."

"Are you serious?" she asked, her voice echoing against the walls and cathedral ceiling. He nodded, his gaze hard, and she suddenly felt very vulnerable. "Does that line often work for you?" she asked casually, attempting to mask her growing anxiety.

He shrugged. "Usually I don't have a problem getting people to do what I want them to do, particularly women." He stepped toward her and crossed his arms. "In fact when I asked my last real estate agent that same question, she took off all her clothes and we screwed in the portico."

"Really?"

He stepped closer. "She made almost twenty thousand dollars on her commission. I'm sure she felt the trade-off was worth it."

"Then maybe you should call her again!"

She smashed the file folders against his chest and headed for the door, papers, photographs and notes spilling onto the beautiful Travertine tile. She charged outside, digging through her purse until she found her phone. She punched in Lorraine's number, and firmly grasped her car key in her hand. When he appeared outside, she placed the key against the hood of the car. At the sight the color drained from his face.

"What are you doing?"

"If you come near me, I'll give your car a memory that'll be very expensive to fix." He put up his hands in defeat and took a step back. She grimaced as she heard the familiar script of Lorraine's voice mail. "Lorraine, I'm with Stan Wertz. He's just propositioned me. Call me when you get this message."

"Ari, I'm sorry," he apologized. "I was way out of line."

"You sure as hell were!"

"Can you please put your keys away? I promise I'm not going to do anything inappropriate. You've made your position quite clear, and while I'm definitely a little surprised that you are rebuffing me, I actually admire your spitfire. But I do have one question for you—why?"

She shook her head, puzzled. "Why what?"

"Why are you refusing me? I mean I'm good looking, in great shape, I'm charming and I'm incredibly wealthy. Where's the turnoff?"

She could see that he was genuinely perplexed. To most women he would be the complete package. The money alone would be incentive to forgive his sleaziness. She put her keys back in her purse and faced him.

"I'm a lesbian," she announced. "Now, you have a choice. You can take me back to my car or we can continue to find you a house without further incident. Which would you prefer, Mr. Wertz?"

A smile spread across his face. "I knew there was a reason." He extended his arm toward the front door. "After you, Ms. Adams."

CHAPTER THIRTEEN

Investigating the disappearance of Selena Diaz consumed much of Molly's morning. A neighbor recalled hearing a motor start in the middle of the night, but no one had seen or heard any activity since then. The landlord was called, a middle-aged slumlord from Scottsdale, who obviously cared little for the property. He'd barely opened the door for Molly and Andre before speeding off in his Mercedes, determined to leave South Phoenix as soon as possible.

They found various possessions that Molly knew wouldn't have been abandoned during a normal move, including a dollhouse that she was sure belonged to Selena. She pictured Maria and Selena spending hours creating stories around the tiny figures now littered haphazardly in front of the structure on the old shag carpet.

"Where do you think they went?" Andre asked.

"Far away. Something scared them enough to get out."

And she wondered if that *something* was actually a *someone*—Hector Cervantes. His alibi for the day of Maria's murder checked out, but she knew there were plenty of Hector's gang buddies who would do anything he said.

As noon approached, Andre went to run errands, and she took a walk to look for the man the Jack in the Box worker had described. She was rather certain he was one of her informants.

The February sun pleasantly warmed the downtown buildings and by lunchtime, the sweaters and coats that had been worn to work were shed across the backs of office chairs.

She strode down Third Avenue, stripping off her suit jacket after the first block. Even in the dead of winter, a laughable expression in Phoenix, the residents could break into a sweat just from a walk. Despite the lack of real seasons it was still better than shoveling snow.

She crossed at the light, passing a sidewalk vendor selling daisies. She debated whether to stop and buy a bouquet for Ari, but they weren't scheduled to be together again until tomorrow night. By then the flowers would wilt, at least a little. Of course she could show up at her place unannounced, but the idea made her uncomfortable. They hadn't deviated from the set schedule since they'd started dating and somehow she thought if she surprised her, it would change the relationship, propelling it into a new dimension that she wasn't sure she could handle.

"Ma'am, can I help you?" a young woman asked.

"No thank you," she quickly responded.

"Are you sure?" a voice asked. She turned to find Franco Perez smelling a bouquet of the dainty white flowers. "They look pretty good."

She aggressively approached Perez, only to have two large men appear from amid the daisy carts and step between her and the gangster. "Are you following me?" she blurted.

He motioned the men away, and they strolled down the sidewalk. She realized how much he looked like his sister. He couldn't be more than nineteen and his baby face betrayed whatever tough act he hoped to convey.

"I want to know if you've found my sister's killer yet."

"I'm not going to discuss a police investigation with you, Franco. When we're ready, we'll arrest someone and your mother will be contacted. If you want any information, you'll need to talk to her."

He offered a slight grin and looked even younger. She couldn't imagine how this boy was Hector Cervantes's fiercest rival. He hardly looked old enough to buy bubblegum. "But since you're here, I have a few questions for you. Your mother says that you're not close with your family anymore. Is that true?"

He frowned. "I'm not close to my mother."

"So you were still seeing Maria?"

"Sometimes. I'll pick her up from school, and we'll have an ice cream." His lip quivered. "At least we used to."

She couldn't help but feel sorry for him. She thought of the photo of the two of them in each other's arms. Whatever he did on the streets didn't involve her. He had the good sense to shield her from that world. "Do you have any idea who killed Maria?"

He shook his head, his eyes downward. "No, but if I did..." He let the thought die and wiped the tears away with his sleeve. When he had composed himself he stared at her, and his youthful face morphed into the hard expression of a gang lord. "You find who did this, Detective, and if it had anything to do with Mayhem Locos, your job will be easier. You just let me know."

"Why would my job be easier?"

With a shrug he was a boy again. His bodyguards appeared next to him, and one of them presented her with a bouquet of daisies. "To show our appreciation," Perez explained. "Find my sister's killer."

"Franco, you need to stay out of this," she warned. "Just let me do my job and quit following me."

He nodded cordially. "Of course, Detective. We have the utmost faith in you, but we'll be close by."

The gang members sauntered down the sidewalk. She tossed the flowers in a nearby trash can and continued for another block until she stood at the edge of Patriots Park. She gazed out at the clusters of business people relaxing on the benches, enjoying their lunches with co-workers or a good book.

She caught sight of a familiar face just beyond the edge of the old courthouse. He was sitting on the ground reading a paperback. From a distance he looked like many of the other lunchtime park dwellers but as she approached, his haggard appearance became obvious. His jeans were faded and the cuffs of his sweatshirt were frayed yet no putrid smell emanated from his body.

Professor Shakespeare ignored her, engrossed in a worn copy of *The Stranger* by Camus. She smiled at his sense of respectability. His shopping cart was well-hidden in the bushes and since he wasn't asleep, she knew no one would complain and the cops would leave him alone.

When the professor finally glanced up, it took a few seconds before recognition crossed his face.

"Detective," he said plainly.

"How are you, Professor Shakespeare?"

"I am filled with joy, gentle friend. And may fresh days of love accompany your heart!"

She smiled. Most of the man's conversations were quotations from Shakespeare's plays and accounted for his unusual street name. She nodded, understanding his meaning and wondering if she looked like a woman in love.

Professor Shakespeare's speckled gray afro swayed in the wind, pressing against the side of his head. His bushy beard needed a trim, but his eyes radiated intelligence. When he smiled, she was greeted by rows of perfect teeth, obviously regularly cleaned and checked. The professor was not what he seemed.

He waited for a response to his quotation and all she could think to say was, "Interesting."

"Yes. To expostulate why day is day and night night, and time is time, were nothing but to waste night, day and time."

She shook her head at his wit. He was her favorite informant because he was so observant, and his mind wasn't fogged by mental illness or drugs. He was one of the smartest men she'd ever met, and she'd heard that he was once the chair of the English department at Stanford University. After he'd engaged in an experiment on homelessness years ago, the story went that he'd grown accustomed to the streets, so enamored by the free life that he abandoned his position and moved to Phoenix where the weather was always warm.

Unlike many of the homeless it was obvious he had a place to sleep each night. Molly suspected the English department chair of Phoenix College, who happened to be one of his former students, had found him a closet somewhere on campus where he could rest at night and spend his days reading, writing and watching people.

"I am certain that you did not seek me out to discuss literature," he continued. "I am not of that feather, to shake off my friend when he must need me."

"I understand that you ate at Jack in the Box on Sunday afternoon."

He sighed deeply. "Ah, yes. I am a great eater of beef, and I believe that it does harm to my wit."

"Somehow I think whichever character said that wasn't referring to a Jumbo Jack, but I think it applies."

He laughed until he cried. "Oh, Detective Nelson, kindness in women, not their beauteous looks, shall win my love."

She always had to read between the lines with him, but she was sure he was affirming her question.

"Did you take your meal to Washington School and eat it?"

His face sobered. "Hell is empty and all the devils here."

"Does that mean you did or didn't go to the drugstore?"

"No! He that filches from me my good name robs me of that which not enriches him but makes me poor indeed."

Molly leaned close to him, invading his personal space. "I need to know how your food receipt for that meal wound up in one of the classrooms at the school. The time you purchased it was only a few minutes before that little girl was killed on the playground. Somebody ate that food at the school and either killed that girl or saw the person who did. Was that *you?*"

His face disintegrated into concern, and he shook his head violently. "No, the purest treasure mortal times afford is a spotless reputation."

"But you heard about the little girl getting killed?"

He nodded and started to cry. "The elements be kind to thee and make thy spirits all of comfort: fare thee well!"

Molly grabbed him by the shoulder until he looked into her eyes. "I need to know right now how that receipt got into the school or I'm taking you in as a murder suspect."

"Men's vows are women's traitors."

"What does that mean? Are you saying some woman betrayed you? Was a woman with you?"

"I have a kind soul that would give you thanks but knows not how to do it except with tears."

Her head was swimming. His quotations were becoming more cryptic with each statement. "Who was it, Professor? I need a name."

He mumbled something indiscernible and buried his head in his hands.

She shook his shoulder and when he raised his head, fear crossed his face. "You need to help me," she said as kindly as she could.

"I know not her name. She wears the coat of a game board."

When he picked up his book again and opened it with a grand gesture, she knew the conversation was over. She trudged back to her car, thinking about his quotations. She almost didn't notice her flat front tire.

"Shit."

She squatted and saw the cause—a switchblade handle protruded between the treads. *Hector Cervantes.*

After the crime scene unit dusted for prints, Andre picked her up and they returned to the school, certain that the relationship between Raul and Maria was critical to the investigation. Someone besides Selena had to know something, and after interviewing five more children before school dismissed at three-thirty, they learned that Maria and Raul's relationship was complicated and had deteriorated even further after they attended the science fair at the Arizona Science Center, the week prior to Maria's death.

"That's when they got *really* mad at each other," Balinda Benson told them. She prided herself as Maria's second best friend, directly under Selena in the hierarchy of school liaisons.

"And I heard something else, too," she whispered, her eyes wide.

"What was that?" Molly asked.

"Selena said that Raul had it bad for Maria."

"Did you believe the rumor?"

"I don't know if it was true. Right after she said it she told me she was just kidding."

"So what do you think? Was it a joke or was it really true?"

Balinda smacked her lips together and swished her legs back and forth. "Don't know. But they sure didn't like each other after the science trip."

"What happened on the science trip?"

She bowed her head. "I didn't get to go."

"Why not?"

"I got in trouble."

"What did you do?"

"I told a lie."

CHAPTER FOURTEEN

Twelve houses and four hours later Wertz was frustrated with the offerings. "Is this all there is? None of them is special," he whined.

Ari nodded sympathetically. She was used to clients showing initial displeasure. "Tell me what these houses don't have that you want."

He looked around the spacious home in which they were standing. It was the nicest and priciest of the ones they'd previewed, sitting at the top of a butte that overlooked North Scottsdale.

"I want something bigger, stylish and unique. I don't want a home that anyone else has." He paced and thought. Suddenly he snapped his fingers and pointed at her. "I want a house worthy of my car."

"Are you prepared to go above your initial price range?"

"Significantly. The Hometown Grocery guy needs an impressive home," he explained as they got back into the roadster.

"So I guess FoodCo won't be buying you out?"

He snarled at the mention of the competition. "FoodCo will never take over my company. Never. I will do whatever it takes to remain an independent. Do you know that the FoodCo chain doesn't offer health benefits to anyone who is part time?"

"Isn't that illegal?"

"Not if you manipulate the workers' schedules carefully. You can stay just within the law and keep the profits lucrative for the people at the top. I pay benefits to all my workers," he added with pride. "We're a family."

The statement had a false ring to it, but she realized the man might be a chauvinist and a good boss as well. Clearly his generosity didn't interfere with his personal wealth or he wouldn't be buying a house three times more expensive than the one he was selling. She thought about some of the other listings available in Desert Mountain. They were top dollar, and she couldn't help but smile over the commission each one guaranteed.

As they wound their way back down the butte, he listed some of the other amenities he wanted. His head whipped to the right, and he snapped the wheel in the same direction, veering up a private drive to an enormous gate. What sat behind the iron bars was an expansive and eye-catching home, literally built into the side of the butte. Its distinctive lines matched those of the mountain. The colors accented the desert landscape that cocooned the walls and roof. Enormous windows gave the owner a breathtaking view of Scottsdale and a bi-level balcony on the side perched over a swimming pool that seemed to disappear into the interior of the house, the mountain or both.

"This is it," he announced.

She shot him a surprised glance. "What are you talking about? This house isn't for sale."

He parted his lips into a devilish smile. "Ari, everything is for sale." He uttered the statement with absolute assuredness. "People buy and sell things at convenience and everyone has a price."

She thought of Edgington's IOU stabbed into the dartboard. "I don't agree with that," she said, shaking her head.

He leaned so close to her that she could feel his breath on her cheek. "For the right amount of money, security or power, I could coerce you to do anything. Anything."

"I don't agree."

He held up a finger. "It's true."

His smug expression revolted her and before she could stop herself, she said, "Did Warren Edgington agree with your business philosophy?"

He blinked, but the rest of his face remained motionless. "Warren? Poor bastard. Why do you mention him?"

Ari shrugged, trying to calm herself. "I saw the two of you arguing at the luncheon and just wondered why you didn't see eye-to-eye."

He laughed. "Warren and I were friends. His mistress was my secretary, Candy. We were arguing because he was going to leave his wife for her, and I was urging him to save his marriage instead." He stared ahead and sighed. "Maybe if I'd tried a little more to help him he wouldn't have... done what he did. There's no reason why he couldn't have kept the wife and still had a little fun on the side."

Ari's disdain grew, and she wanted nothing more than to escape the car and put as much distance as possible between them. He had no scruples. She'd worked with real estate agents with questionable ethics, but he was a snake.

Realizing she needed to get off the mountain she took a breath and said tactfully, "I just don't see it that way, Stan. I have most everything I want for myself. I'm very happy, and I don't have a price."

"What about for someone else? Your price doesn't have to benefit yourself. Even if there is nothing you personally desired, if I could guarantee the happiness or success of a loved one then you might consider it, wouldn't you?"

Ari turned away and for a fleeting moment she wished that money could bring her mother and brother back or give Molly the confidence to see their love was real.

He draped his arm around her. "Look up this house and see

who owns it. Ask them what they think it's worth and offer it. If they hesitate, double the price."

"What if they don't want to sell?"

"Well," he said, as he maneuvered the roadster back down the hill, "there are always other methods of persuasion."

He dropped her at the front of his house and sped off to work. The weight of his words lingered in her ears. She wondered if she were that rich, would she really go to any lengths to remain wealthy and powerful? She wanted to believe she was incapable of such unscrupulous behavior but she knew money changed people, and she was hesitant to declare she was immune from its temptations.

She checked her watch and realized she only had ten minutes until her appointment with Biz and the manager of Trombetta Dwellings. She sped down Seventh Avenue, timing the lights at forty miles an hour. Soon she was surrounded by the glass and brick of the downtown skyscrapers and the crisscrossing one-way streets. She navigated the turns until she came to the circular driveway in front of the city's most innovative loft property. A valet appeared at her door, and she stepped out with her briefcase, offering him the keys to the 4Runner.

The lobby was bustling with activity as local business people enjoyed their lunches at The Sidewinder Deli, sat atop the shoeshine chairs reading their newspapers or tapped away on their laptops at the workstations that lined the enormous windows around the entire space. She spotted the elevators for the private residences behind a sliding glass entryway with a doorman hunkered over a marble counter. When the doors parted as she entered, the doorman, a tall, muscular Hispanic man, stood and smiled.

"Welcome to Trombetta Dwellings. How may I assist you?"

"I'm Ari Adams, a real estate agent, and I have an appointment with Terry Lancer."

The doorman nodded and picked up the phone while she looked around the quiet waiting area, a stark contrast to the noise of the outer lobby. She heard the whoosh of the glass doors again and Biz appeared beside her, wearing tight jeans and a Rolling Stones T-shirt.

"I already love it," she whispered. "And I haven't even seen the place."

"It's really something, isn't it?"

A lock clicked, and Terry Lancer emerged through a door she'd missed because it blended into the wall. Dressed in a suit with French cuffs, she realized the man's haircut probably cost more than the entire outfit she was wearing. He smiled broadly, his gorgeous white teeth in contrast to his dark tan.

"Ms. Adams," he said extending his hand, "I'm Terry Lancer."

"Very nice to meet you, Mr. Lancer. This is my client, Elizabeth Stone."

The warmth exuding from Lancer turned up a notch as he greeted Biz. "Such a pleasure, Ms. Stone. Welcome to Trombetta Dwellings."

"Thank you," she said.

"Shall we go up and look at an available residence?"

He motioned to the elevators and one magically opened, but Ari realized it was the doing of the ever-observant doorman. They glided up to the twelfth floor and found themselves standing in another lobby with hallways extending left and right.

Lancer took the lead, and they followed him down the west corridor as he spoke of the building's history with passionate interest. Biz asked questions intermittently and Lancer always knew the answers. When he opened the door to 1209 he stopped talking and allowed them to take in the space. Six large glass windows spanned the southern wall, a throwback to its days as a machine factory when sunlight was critical to the workers' productivity.

She watched Biz's reactions to the kitchen area, the enormous elevated living space and the spacious bathroom done entirely in chrome. She loved the look, the contemporary fixtures and design accenting the historic old structure. Biz's expression remained neutral as she explored while Lancer periodically noted features and commented on the living community. He spoke so effortlessly and so unlike a salesman that Ari was impressed.

"Is this the nicest unit available?" Biz asked suddenly.

"Um, well, what exactly are you looking for, Ms. Stone?" he asked, clearly surprised.

She glanced around, her hands on her hips. "Well, I'd like a northern exposure instead of southern, a corner unit, preferably one with more square footage, and I'll need a bigger kitchen that has an island to accommodate my cooking hobby. Is something like that available?"

He furrowed his brow. "We do have a corner unit on the fifteenth floor that's three hundred square feet larger with a beautiful view of Piestewa Peak, at least when the pollution's down. But it's much more expensive, and I'm afraid the kitchen is identical."

She studied the area carefully. "How hard would it be to remodel the kitchen to my specifications?"

He smiled slightly and bowed his head. "Assuming that you abide by the CCRs we've established, it's only as difficult as the price of your contractor."

"Let's go see it."

The surprised expression returned to Lancer's face, and Ari immediately touched her arm. "Are you sure about this, Biz? It could be horribly expensive."

She laughed and squeezed her hand. "Another reason I'm an appealing catch is that I have some money." When Ari continued to look worried, she added, "Just think of your commission. Shall we go?"

CHAPTER FIFTEEN

Molly savored her third scotch during the crowded happy hour at Hideaway. Several women had hit on her, and she'd politely rebuffed all of them. All she wanted was Ari. When the drums of *Wipeout* burst from her cell phone, she almost cried out in joy.

"Hi."

"Where are you?" Ari whispered seductively.

"I'm still at work," she lied.

"Do you have much more to do or can you leave soon?"

She closed her eyes, listening to the soothing lilt of her voice.

"Honey?" Ari chuckled. "Are you falling asleep?"

She shook her head and blinked, realizing the third scotch was probably a mistake. "No, babe, I'm here."

Ari sighed. "Hey, would you like to come over?"

She sat up, surprised.

"I mean, I know it's not our night, but we missed last night and I'd really like to see you, if you want. I'll totally understand if you're too tired or if you'd rather stick to the schedule…"

Her voice trailed off in mid-speech. When she finally comprehended everything Ari had said, she realized that at some point she'd started smiling.

"Honey?" Ari asked gently. "Um, well, we can do this another time."

"No!" she shouted. She took a breath to control her voice. "No, I'd really like to see you."

"Oh, great. Then why don't you come over to my place? I'll put together a light supper. Will that be okay?"

"Fine. I'll stop at my apartment and be over by seven-thirty."

She quickly hung up and downed a glass of water, working to shed the drunken state that was gripping her. Normally she'd nurse a cup of coffee for at least another hour before she attempted to drive, but she desperately wanted Ari—now.

She navigated the streets, careful not to blow through any lights or stop signs. She was five blocks from her apartment when flashing lights appeared behind her. *Shit.* She pulled over and checked her appearance in the mirror. As long as they didn't give her a Breathalyzer, she'd be okay.

"Evening, ma'am. You appeared to be weaving. Have you been drinking?" the uniformed officer asked.

She showed him her badge and shrugged. "Just a couple, officer. I'm on my way home now."

He studied her badge and nodded. "I've heard of you, Detective Nelson. You're working the Maria Perez murder, aren't you?"

"Yeah, me and my partner, Andre Williams."

The officer grinned. "I know Andre. We play ball on Saturdays." He handed back her badge and nodded seriously. "Get home, okay?"

"Thanks," she said with great relief. It wasn't until he'd driven away that her heart stopped pounding.

As she pulled into her assigned parking space, she noticed her neighbor Dorothy Lyons approaching. Dorothy pulled her metal cart that usually hauled laundry, but tonight it was full of feathers.

"Howdy, neighbor," Dorothy said with a mischievous grin.

"Hey, what are you up to?"

She stepped in front of the cart and whistled. "Nothing, officer. I'm just a little old lady out for a walk."

Molly pointed at the feathers. "And what are those for?"

"Promise you won't arrest me?"

She laughed at the idea. Dorothy was a spitfire, and she thought of her as family. "I'm off duty," she said, "unless you're murdering someone by feathering them to death. What's up?"

Dorothy looked around the parking lot and stepped closer. "I'm gonna teach Howard Birnbaum some manners. He's parked in my space for the last time."

She nodded, well aware of Dorothy's ongoing battle with their inconsiderate and crotchety neighbor who refused to park in his assigned space, taking whichever one was open and closest to the building. Of course he'd never taken her spot, probably because he knew she'd throw a boot over his rear wheel.

Dorothy reached underneath the feathers, some of which were spilling onto the ground, and pulled out a can of shaving cream. "I'm just gonna tar and feather his windshield a little. That's not illegal, is it?"

She laughed and shook her head. "Nope. Just do a good job."

"You wanna help?"

"I probably shouldn't. I'm on my way to Ari's."

Dorothy smiled. Molly knew how much she liked Ari, and the fact that the older lady approved of their relationship was a bonus. "Say hi from me. She's a great kid. I want to have you both over again for supper."

"That sounds great."

"Okay. I'm off to commit public mayhem. If this doesn't work, can I borrow a taser?"

She realized too late that she could've used a shower, and she kicked herself for appearing at Ari's door smelling like stale cigarettes and scotch. As usual Ari looked amazing in jeans and a long-sleeved T-shirt. Her hair was up in a bun, the way she preferred it. Unable to be physically apart from her for another second, she immediately pulled her into an embrace and a rough kiss. Each murmured her own penance for the fight before her tongue silenced their lips. The taste of Ari's mouth only heightened her passion which was a razor sharp edge of desire.

"I need a shower. Take a shower with me," she pleaded.

Without acknowledging the request Ari stepped away and went to the kitchen. She turned off the stove and removed the small pot from the hot burner.

"So you're not hungry?" she teased.

"I'm very hungry."

Ari smiled seductively and crossed the distance between them, discarding her T-shirt on the couch and stepping out of her jeans while Molly bit her lip in anticipation. "What do you want to eat?" she asked innocently, batting her eyes for dramatic effect.

"What are you offering?" Molly parlayed, watching as she unhooked the clasp of her bra. When it fell to the floor their eyes met.

Ari licked her lips. "Well, I thought about soup and sandwiches, but I don't think you're interested."

"No."

"Would you like me to undress you, Detective? I can smell that suit from here."

She quickly shed her clothes, all the while staring into her eyes, which seemed to sparkle.

They drifted together for another kiss. Ari was the best kisser she'd ever met, crafting each kiss perfectly. She knew when to be rough, when to tease and when to be tender. These were the kisses of forgiveness and caring.

Ari took her hand and pulled her into the bathroom, reaching for the hot water tap. Clad only in their underwear, they touched and explored each other until their bodies were slick and wet from the shower steam. Ari stepped into the shower and crooked her finger at Molly who followed behind. She backed into the corner and laced her fingers behind her head.

Molly fell to her knees, her hands trailing down Ari's chest, her fingertips lingering on her nipples while she kissed her soft belly. Ari moaned softly and dropped her hands into Molly's curls.

"Now," she begged.

Molly became easily frustrated by her uncooperative, wet underwear and tore them away before she spread her legs and kissed her thighs tenderly.

Only when they'd pleasured each other long enough for the hot water to run cold did they retreat to the warmth of Ari's expensive sheets, allowing the fine linen and their body heat to dry them. Ari fell asleep, but Molly awoke frequently, remaining in her embrace for as long as she could, unwilling to break the physical connection that healed their anger. The emotional anxiety remained, as it always did after they made love.

Eventually the images of Maria Perez's autopsy filled her head, and she headed for the kitchen and the bottle of scotch Ari kept above the sink for her. She knew her drinking worried Ari, and it secretly worried her too, but she was certain she could control it. She wandered through the living room, settling into Ari's desk chair. She turned on the computer, deciding to surf the net for 6815. Maybe she'd get lucky.

While she waited for the machine to start up, her gaze strayed to the stack of Ari's client folders that always sat on the edge of the desk. She smiled at her impeccable organization, until she noticed Biz Stone's name on one of them.

CHAPTER SIXTEEN

Ari maneuvered through the small parking lot of Susan's Diner searching for an empty space. After three tries she swore and parked on the nearby side street. She trudged back to the building, her anger growing with each step. She'd agreed to meet her father here for breakfast, but that was before she'd woken up and faced Molly's drunken, jealous rage.

Molly had found Biz's client file during the night and instead of waking her up so they could talk about it rationally, she'd chosen to stew in her anger, polishing off an entire bottle of scotch in the process. Only when dawn broke did Molly shake her awake, thrusting the file in her face.

"What the hell is this?"

It had taken a minute for her world to realign. The ugly, twisted face that hovered over her was nearly unrecognizable.

The gears in her brain unlocked and the scene finally registered.

"I was going to tell you—"

"When? After you'd finished the deal? Or after you two had slept together?"

"Honey, I wanted to tell you last night, but we were a little preoccupied. I didn't think it was appropriate."

Molly threw the file against the wall, and Ari jumped. She'd never seen Molly like this, although she'd admitted to a violent past with her other lovers.

"Telling me wasn't the issue. Why is Biz your client? You know how I feel about her, and you know how she feels about you."

"It's just a business arrangement—"

"Bullshit! Don't insult me. That woman wants you, and I'm beginning to wonder if the feeling is mutual."

She automatically shook her head and touched her arm. "Baby, you're drunk. You're not rational. Don't say that. Don't think that."

Molly shoved her—hard—and the force propelled her on her back. She lay on the bed, momentarily out of breath. Molly had never touched her in anger, and she fought back tears.

"Don't tell me what to think!" Molly screamed.

She stormed out of the room, and Ari heard the sounds of her making coffee. She imagined Molly would consume an entire pot to quell her hangover before she went to work. The clock read seven-fifteen, and she suddenly remembered her breakfast date with her father. She quickly got ready and when she emerged from the bedroom, she found her sprawled across the couch, a cold pack over her eyes.

"I have to meet my father for breakfast. Are you okay?"

"Never better," she slurred. "Oh, and do give your father my love," she added. "Wait, you can't. He doesn't know I exist."

She wanted to go to Molly, but her hands were shaking. For the first time she was afraid of what Molly might do. She chose to stay by the door. "Baby, I'm so sorry," she said.

Molly sprang up and headed for the bedroom, slamming the door behind her.

She called her father's cell several times in an attempt to cancel, but it only went to voice mail. Worried that he'd never get the messages she felt obligated to appear.

She found him in a booth chatting up the waitress who topped off his coffee. When he glanced in her direction she pasted on a pleasant smile for his benefit.

"Hi, honey. How about some coffee?"

She nodded, and the waitress filled her cup while she settled into the seat across from him. She didn't bother to pick up a menu, her emotions killing her appetite.

Jack frowned. "You're not eating."

"I'm not hungry."

He said nothing else and continued to study the entrees. When the waitress returned to take the order he glanced at her, but she looked away.

They sat in silence, Ari avoiding his stare. He drummed his fingers on the Formica tabletop and she noticed his wedding ring. He and her mother had divorced several years before her mother's death, but she couldn't remember him wearing his ring—not even at her funeral.

"Not that I think you'll tell me," he said, interrupting her thoughts, "but just so you know your old man is somewhat observant and his memory is unaffected by his age, I'll ask you what's wrong."

"I'm okay."

"Nope, I disagree. When you skip breakfast something's buggin' you. That's how your mother and I survived your teenage years. She'd serve a plate of eggs and if you didn't eat, I'd quietly excuse myself so the two of you could talk." He chuckled. "You were the only kid I knew who'd eat eggs at seven at night except when you were hurting." He paused and sighed. "I guess we can't count on your mom's help here anymore."

Her eyes dropped to the table as she willed herself not to cry. "There's just some stuff going on right now," she said simply.

"Work stuff or personal stuff?"

"Both, I guess. More personal stuff."

She looked into his eyes and saw none of the hatred and

judgment that she remembered from the past, from the night he had disowned her and banished her from the house. In the end it had been his undoing. He lost his daughter and his wife, who divorced him soon after.

She couldn't erase the memory completely, but she felt compelled to take a step forward, not for him but for Molly. She owed him nothing and Molly everything.

"Actually, Dad, there's someone in my life. Someone important."

A tentative smile crossed his face. "I'm glad. What does she do?"

"She's a cop."

He didn't look surprised. "Does she work downtown?"

"Uh-huh."

"What division?"

"I don't want to go into it yet. I'm not ready for you to meet her."

He patted her hand. "I'm sure whatever's going on will work out."

She smiled in relief, grateful for the words even if she wasn't sure he was right.

The subject dropped when his breakfast appeared. He pointed to his plate with his fork. "You sure you don't want any?"

She shook her head and watched him shovel the food into his mouth in typical cop mode. Her mother had berated him endlessly for his poor table manners, certain that Ari and her brother Richie would follow suit.

"Sol and I went to the Suns game last night. Double overtime."

"Great," she said with little enthusiasm. "Did they win?"

"Oh, yeah. Steve Nash nailed a jumper with two seconds left. It was just beautiful."

Ari grinned. They'd found some neutral ground. They spent fifteen minutes talking basketball, the Phoenix Suns and Jack's adopted team, the Portland Trailblazers.

"Can I ask you something as a cop?"

He took a sip of coffee and looked at her thoughtfully, obviously surprised by the abrupt shift in the conversation. She figured if she couldn't talk to Molly about her suspicions, he was the next best person.

"Did you ever just have a hunch that someone had committed a crime but you couldn't prove it?"

He snorted and shook his head. "Happens all the time. I probably had a hundred cases where I knew the perp, but I couldn't prove it." He leaned closer and pointed a finger at her. "One time the guy actually confessed to me after the judge threw out the case."

Ari's eyes widened. "What did you do?"

Jack cleared his throat and adopted a proper expression. "As an officer sworn to uphold the law and live by judicial ethics there wasn't anything I could do."

She knew her father better, and her raised eyebrow told him so.

"Actually he had an unfortunate run of bad luck when he got nailed for breaking and entering. Wound up in the joint because of his priors and some of his old friends put a shiv in his back."

"I suppose that's karma at work."

"Exactly." He paused and said, "So why are you askin'?"

"I have this client who's the sleaziest person I've ever met. I think he's capable of most anything."

"What do you think he did?"

She hesitated. If she told him the truth, he'd run to Sol and Molly immediately and she'd look like a fool. She had no proof. Until she got some there wasn't anything to investigate.

"I'm not really sure, fraud at least."

"Well, my best advice is to keep watching and listening. Most criminals make mistakes, and if they think they're hot shit they tend to make *more* mistakes."

She nodded. "Thanks. That's good advice."

His face brightened. "Really? A compliment? I think I'm blushing."

The check came, and the conversation dwindled as they drifted out to the parking lot in silence.

Jack finally said, "I'd really like to see you once more before I leave on Friday, maybe Jane too."

She stuffed her hands into the pockets of her jacket. "I'm not sure. I'll have to check my schedule and ask Jane."

His expression suggested he knew he was getting the brush-off. "Sure. I understand. Three meals in a week after a four year absence is probably pushing it."

Ari snorted. "Dad, it's not that—"

"Of course it is, honey. And that's okay. It's just that eventually I want us to get to the point where we're gonna say everything that needs to be said."

Ari shrugged. "Why?"

"Why?" he repeated, clearly stunned.

"I mean, I think that parts of the past are best left there. I don't want to go back."

"I know that, honey," he said gently. "But I want us to move forward. You're all I have."

His words hung in the air as a group of women walked between them and dissolved the conversation.

"Look, Dad, I'll call you tomorrow, okay?"

She turned and walked away, almost disappointed when he didn't call to her.

A throng of sixth-graders passed Ari as she strolled toward One Desert Plaza, the home of the Hometown Grocery Corporation and Stan Wertz's executive office. Located near the Arizona Science Center and Heritage Square, the three entities made for eclectic partners. The Science Center and Heritage Square were major draws for tourists and students, the technology of the future literally a stone's throw away from the series of incredible homes from the late 1880's, which now served as businesses or museums.

She glanced toward the Teeter House and smiled. She had wonderful memories of her mother taking her there for tea and cookies. Those were the most precious times of her life, remembering the two of them sitting in their best outfits—they always dressed up to go to tea—and her mother giggling and making up stories about the people who passed by. She blinked away some tears and took a deep breath, feeling overwhelmed. After years of being isolated and apart from family, she'd had breakfast with her father and vivid memories of her mother all in the same morning.

She found a bench and sat down for a moment. Stan Wertz could wait. She glanced at the parking garage where only a week ago she'd found Warren Edgington in his car with the shiny tower nearby. How difficult it would be for Wertz to kill Edington and get back to his office? But he had no motive that she could find and if anything, it looked like they were friends. He'd never had any business dealings with Edgington. And could someone force you to drink alcohol and drugs? How would he do that? There'd been no signs of struggle. None of it made sense, and she knew she was probably allowing her hatred to cloud her judgment. She *wanted* him to be guilty of something, but she wanted her commission too.

She rose and strolled purposefully through the front doors of the enormous office complex. It didn't surprise her that his offices covered the entire top floor of the building, and the ride up the twenty-two stories made her ears pop. The elevator opened directly in front of a receptionist who sat behind a massive mahogany desk. She waited patiently noticing that every stick of furniture and every piece of equipment was top dollar.

"Ms. Adams, please take this corridor to the first desk you see," the receptionist said pleasantly. She pointed to Ari's right but dared not leave her post.

She only glanced at one of the Hometown Grocery photos that lined the hallway, unwilling to look at endless pictures of Stan Wertz. She arrived in front of a petite woman in a very expensive silk blouse. Her brown hair cascaded around her face and Ari thought she should be in a shampoo commercial. The woman looked up from her computer with a pleasant smile.

"You must be Ms. Adams, Mr. Wertz's real estate agent. I'm Candy, Mr. Wertz's personal assistant. Let me show you in."

Ari realized this was the woman who'd had an affair with Warren Edgington. Did she still care for him? Certainly she wouldn't give a false alibi for Wertz if she did.

They approached the expansive oak door. Candy cleared her

throat and prepared to knock. It was as if she was rehearsing for the simple task of announcing a visitor, and she was worried that she wouldn't get it right. When her knuckles finally touched the door, she paused and waited for permission to enter the inner sanctum. They took a few steps inside, Wertz appearing not to notice them, his gaze focused on the enormous computer monitor that sat on his desk.

"I'll be with you in a moment," he said gruffly. "Look around. Candy, honey, will you get me a gin and tonic? Ari, what would you like? I've got everything you could imagine and Candy's first career was as a bartender. She's a wiz."

Candy rolled her eyes, and Ari suppressed a chuckle. "I'd just like a sparkling water," she answered.

Candy busied herself behind the bar while she strolled around his office, stopping in front of a model that sat in the center of the room. *Hometown City Center* was written in block lettering in the lower left corner. No wonder the building was so much bigger than a Hometown Grocery. She remembered the article she'd read online and Wertz's desire to rival the big box stores. She saw the streets that bordered the store—Elliott and Alma School—one of the busiest corners in Chandler, a neighboring suburb of Phoenix.

She turned her thoughts to business and seated herself on his expensive leather sofa. She pulled several files from her briefcase and strategically arranged them on the glass coffee table so that he could see the variety of houses from which he could choose. She'd spent the entire morning creating color-coded portfolios for each price range, and she'd included several glossy photos of each property and its amenities, hoping he could be distracted from the house at the top of the butte.

Candy took his drink to his desk and brought her the sparkling water in a crystal glass, setting it delicately on a handcrafted ivory coaster. When Ari looked up, she flashed a seductive smile and touched her shoulder. "Would you like anything else?"

She shook her head, but Candy continued to hover, exposing her cleavage and the hot pink bra that held it all in place. Her smile broadened when she realized Ari had indeed noticed her perfect breasts, and she squeezed her shoulder. "Let me know if you change your mind. I make an incredible margarita."

She smiled pleasantly and watched her sashay out of the office. She sipped her water and glanced at Wertz, his hands flying across the keyboard while he stared intently at the screen. He smacked the last key with a deliberate stroke and rose from his chair. Instead of immediately joining her, he tugged at the tailored cuffs of his dress shirt, straightened his tie and put on his suit jacket as though he were changing his image before beginning their meeting.

"I'm in a great mood, Ari," he announced. "By this time next year the Hometown City Center will be open, and FoodCo will be crying their eyes out. You're looking at a man who staged a major coup."

"Really?" she said, hoping she looked appropriately interested. "How's that?"

"I got the last great piece of commercial real estate in Chandler. FoodCo wanted it, but I got it. That new center will totally shift the demographics in my favor. I will dominate that area and FoodCo will be lucky to turn a profit."

"How did you manage to pull that off?"

She knew the surveyors for large companies were always a step ahead of the smaller ones because they often had inside information from city planners and real estate brokers. If he'd bested FoodCo he needed leverage.

"Persuasion," he said slyly. "I beat them because I am truly more persuasive." He joined her on the sofa and set his drink on the coffee table. "What did you learn about the house I want?"

She chuckled and picked up the first stack of folders. "Well, I did inquire and I do have some information, but why don't we go through these possibilities first since they're already for sale?"

He immediately shook his head. "Ari, I thought I was clear. There's no other house. I appreciate your effort with this presentation and you obviously do your homework, but I am only interested in that property."

She realized he was adamant and she gently dropped the stack of folders onto the coffee table. "Okay," she said hesitantly. She pulled a thin manila folder from her briefcase and handed it to him. He scanned the contents while she summarized from memory. "The place is so expensive that it has a name, Serendipity. It's a one-of-a-kind built in the Seventies by an architect who was a protégé of Frank Lloyd Wright—"

"That's not surprising," he interrupted. "You could see the Wright influence all over it. Did this guy study at Taliesin West?"

She nodded at his reference to the architectural school located in Scottsdale. "Anyway, the architect, a guy named August Glick, is dead now and the house is owned by his brother, Jacob."

"Have you contacted him?"

"Um, no, not yet. Stan, did you notice what the assessed value is for this house?"

He laughed and went to his desk. "It's only money." He punched a button and Candy's voice filled the office, asking what she could do to help. "Please locate the phone number for Jacob Glick, call him and tell him that I wish to visit him as soon as possible."

Wertz spelled the last name and gave Candy the address for Serendipity. Ari could feel a headache coming on. He had tunnel vision about this house, a place that was unattainable in her estimation. He returned to his desk chair and stared at the monitor.

"You don't think he'll see me, do you?" he challenged, his fingers once again pounding the computer keyboard.

"I'm doubtful," she admitted.

"Ye of little faith. Would you like to make a bet on it?"

Her eyes narrowed. "What kind of bet?"

"Not what you're thinking. I've learned my lesson, Ms. Adams. If I win you let me take you to dinner."

"And if I win?"

"I'll double your commission, whatever it is."

She figured even if she lost, a chance at a doubled commission would be worth a dinner with him.

"I'll take that bet but only if you let me pick the restaurant on the off chance I lose."

"Fine, but every entrée on the menu must be at least twenty-five dollars. You're not taking me to a fast food place," he said.

"Deal."

"You have no idea how amazing Candy can be," he laughed.

"I think I can imagine it," she murmured under her breath. She gathered the file folders into her briefcase and stood to leave. "Well, call me if she gets the meeting."

"Wait. I'll be dialing your cell phone before you hit the ground floor."

She ignored the advice and reached for the doorknob just as Candy came over the speaker. "Mr. Wertz? Mr. Glick said he would meet with you and Ms. Adams tomorrow evening at eight-thirty."

CHAPTER SEVENTEEN

Andre met Molly at her office door. He must have read her expression and chose to take the chair furthest from her desk. She wondered if he could tell that she was nursing a killer hangover or if she still looked drunk. She certainly felt tipsy, and she cursed herself silently. She'd kept drinking into the early morning hours, and even her high tolerance for alcohol couldn't completely mask the effects. She sipped her coffee for another fifteen minutes before she finally looked at him hoping she didn't reek of liquor and that he didn't get too close to notice.

"What have you got?"

"Two things. We may have a lead on Selena Diaz's family, and I think I know what your friend Professor Shakespeare was talking about."

"Good. I have no idea what a game board coat would look like," she said.

He set a checkerboard on her desk. The recognition was instantaneous.

"The person's wearing a red and black flannel jacket. Is that what you think?"

He nodded. "I realized it last night when my nephew wanted to play chess with me. This has to be it, Mol."

"Okay, good job. Now all we need to do is scour the area for a street person that fits that description."

He shrugged. "It shouldn't be that hard."

She handed the checkerboard back to him. "I wouldn't say that out loud."

A knock sounded and Sol Gardener appeared with David Ruskin. "Detectives, I thought I'd stop by and see how we're doing."

She prayed her eyes weren't as bloodshot as she thought.

Andre jumped in to help. "We've got a lead on a possible eyewitness, and we think we've located Maria Perez's best friend. The family's been missing for two days."

Sol nodded, his eyes focused on her. "Nelson, are you okay?"

"I'm fine, sir," she replied, hoping her voice was even.

"Jesus, Nelson, you're drunk!" Ruskin shouted.

She resisted the urge to crush her palms over her ears and glared at him. She said nothing, determined not to lie to Sol.

"David, will you and Andre please excuse us?" Sol asked quietly.

The men left, and he perched on the edge of her desk. "Hey, I know things are tough right now. Ari's dealing with her dad, you're working a terrible murder case. I get it."

At the mention of Ari she almost wailed in pain. When she could finally meet his gaze without bursting into tears, she looked up into his kind eyes and returned his sad smile. "I'm sorry. It'll never happen again."

"It can't," he said firmly.

Although she'd been directed to go home, Molly convinced Andre that all she needed was a run to Starbucks before they continued with their day. On the way he told her about Selena Diaz.

"I'm hearing rumors from one of my informants that her father may owe a loan shark."

"Okay," she said, washing down three more aspirin with her coffee. "Let's visit Hector and then look for the eyewitness."

"And I may have found something on the spreadsheet."

"What?"

"There's a few addresses that I'm certain are owned by dummy corporations. I'd say at least four of the houses are illegal fronts."

She snorted. "Only four?"

He grinned. "Surprising, huh? I think we should focus on those. Separate the legal from the shady. Maybe one of them will go somewhere."

He showed her the list he'd made in his notebook. None of the names was significant and most appeared insignificant. *That's the point.*

"Good work, Andre. Thanks."

"No problem." He glanced at her, a worried look on his face. "Are you sure you're up for this? I'm not happy about defying the chief's direct orders."

"Don't worry about it. If we get in trouble I'll say I kidnapped you at gunpoint."

The smell of rubber permeated every corner of Sandor's Auto World. Molly and Andre wandered to the front counter where Hector Cervantes sat on a stool playing a game on his cell phone. He glanced up at them but didn't blink an eye when Andre hefted her gouged radial onto the counter.

"I'm having a little problem with this tire, Hector," she said.

"Can you tell me what's wrong with it?" She pushed her finger through the punctured sidewall for emphasis.

Cervantes just stared at her. "It seems to me you already have an idea, detective."

"What I'd like to know is how it got this way."

He peered at the slice and grimaced. "I'd say you ran over something, possibly a piece of sharp metal lying in the road?"

Her anger flared, and she hurled the tire across the counter, sending a display of key rings crashing to the floor. Three technicians appeared from the service area but quickly disappeared at the sight of Andre's badge. She leaned over the counter and faced him.

"We're done with the bullshit games. You think you can scare me? Not on your life. What you're going to give me right now is some cooperation. I'm well aware that your Uncle Sandor is using this place to launder drug money. With one phone call from me, the county attorney will be here with a warrant, analyzing every record, every file and every transaction your uncle has made. I'm pretty sure Aunt Claudia can't support her five children while her husband rots in a prison cell. So are you going to talk to me or not?"

Cervantes's eyes conveyed hatred but respect for his adversary. "What do you want to know?"

"Where is Selena Diaz's family?"

"Gone."

"Where?"

"If they're smart, far away from Big Paddy."

She blinked and glanced at Andre. Big Paddy was a loan shark. "What does Paddy have to do with any of this?"

"Pops is in deep. He loves the track, and he owes Paddy a ton of money."

"So their disappearance didn't have anything to do with Maria Perez's murder?" Andre asked.

"No," Cervantes said, clearly annoyed. He glanced at both of them. "What? You thought *I* had something to do with it?" He sat down on his stool and folded his arms. "That's ripe." He looked out at the street and his eyes narrowed. "What do you want with Selena, anyway?"

Molly shook her head. "I'm not at liberty to discuss an ongoing homicide investigation, particularly with a person of interest. I do have a few more questions for you. I've heard that your brother and Maria might actually have been an item. Any truth to that?"

He laughed out loud and shook his head.

"What did Raul tell you?" she pressed.

"Well, I'm not going to tell you anything between *hijos*, but he told me Maria was off right before she died. She acted like she was spooked or something. She'd changed."

"What else did he say?"

"Nothing you need to know." Cervantes motioned to the destroyed radial still teetering on the end of the counter. "Do you want me to do anything with that? I'll fix it for you cheap, considering you're a member of the law enforcement community."

They headed for the door. "No, you keep it. We already dusted it for prints." She pushed on the rickety old handle and turned back to him. "And tell your friend Pablo Nedolo to stay the hell away from my car or he'll spend the best years of his life in the state pen."

Whatever levity that had passed between them was gone and the stone cold face of a gang member met her gaze and nodded slightly.

The Greyhound bus station was their third stop. A young security guard named Bruce confirmed that they were probably looking for a woman nicknamed Checkers.

"I'm sure she'll be by in a day or two," he said. "She never stays away long. I always have to ask her to leave, in a nice way," he added quickly. "She's a great lady, and I wonder what she was like in her old life before her mind went."

"What's wrong with her mind?" Andre asked suspiciously.

"I'm not a doctor, but I'm guessing she suffers from Alzheimer's. She's not very clear about a lot of things. Just the other day she was trying to convince me that the woman on the TV, the news anchor, was her daughter. Go figure!"

"Do you know where else she goes?" Molly interjected.

Bruce sighed. "Hmm, that's a hard one. I'm not sure she's ever mentioned another place. I'd try the streets down by the arena. Sometimes I see her with a soft drink from the arena food court."

The US Airways Arena concourse was crowded with lunchtime traffic. They searched the fast food lines as they crawled toward the counters filled with business people checking their watches. There was no sign of a woman in a red and black plaid coat.

"I'll hit the bathrooms," Molly said. "You go back outside and see if she's on the patio."

They went in separate directions, and she found the ladies' room. Two women were reapplying their lipstick in front of the mirror and only one stall was in use. She squatted down and peered at the shoes, gaining the stares of the women at the sink counters.

"It's okay, I'm a police officer," she announced.

She quickly exited the bathroom certain that the brown penny loafers she'd seen didn't belong to Checkers. There was one more bathroom at the other end of the concourse. She threaded her way through the large crowd toward the entrance. A flash of red caught her attention and a red and black plaid jacket emerged from the bathroom and ducked out a nearby exit where Andre hopefully waited.

By the time Molly reached the door Andre and Checkers were coming back inside, a smile plastered across the old woman's face.

"Detective Nelson, this is my new friend, Checkers." Checkers nodded and pointed at the pizza place in front of them. "I promised Checkers that if she answered a few of our questions, I'd spring for lunch. Does that sound good?"

"I'll get us a table," Molly offered.

She watched the two of them converse, Checkers doing most of the talking and gesturing with her hands. She imagined that by the time they got through the line Andre would know her life story. He was good at drawing people out, talking to them about themselves, unlike Molly who struggled with communication and despised chit chat. Ari often teased her about her inability to hold up her end of their conversations although she knew she was more comfortable with Ari than she'd ever been with anyone. For Ari she had lowered her defenses and exposed her vulnerabilities.

She shifted in the chair remembering their fight that morning. She'd shoved Ari, and she'd seen the fear in her eyes. It made her sick to her stomach. She glanced at Andre and Checkers, who now stood at the front of the line, laughing heartily together. When the food arrived she had no appetite and was content to listen while Andre questioned Checkers.

"Laurie was an amazing child. She was so beautiful, and she had so many friends. All the girls wanted to come over and play dollies with my Laurie." She buried her face in her hands. "I ruined it. I ruined everything."

"How'd you do that?" Andre asked gently.

Checkers sniffled quietly and wiped her nose on her napkin. "I left. I couldn't handle being a mother."

"I'm sure she's forgiven you," he said.

Molly wasn't as optimistic since she was witnessing what a slow, painful process it was for Ari to allow her father back into her life.

He touched her coat, hoping to shift the conversation to business. "Ma'am, we need to ask you about the shooting that happened at the old school two days ago."

Her face went white, and she bolted from the concourse. Molly and Andre scrambled to follow right behind her. She lost her bearings outside and turned in circles, a look of terror on her face. Andre quickly led her to a cement bench on a quiet patch of grass away from the noon hour traffic.

"So bad. So horrible," she mumbled, bringing her hand to cover her mouth, as though she had said too much. The frail fingers were the texture of crepe paper and her whole body shook violently. They waited patiently for her to regain her composure. When her body stilled Andre put a reassuring arm around her shoulder.

"Checkers, did you touch the blood?"

She shook her head and clucked her tongue repeatedly. "I saw it."

"Was that when you were eating your hamburger in the old classroom?"

Checkers gazed up at him as if he were a clairvoyant. "No, I saw the blood when I went down on the playground. She looked like she was sleeping in a red circle. On *Law and Order* when there's blood, somebody's dead. I knew when I saw her body that she was gone."

"Did you know her?"

"I saw her once in a while. She and her little friend loved to play on the old jungle gym. They hung upside down, giggling and laughing at each other. Just the way my Laurie did."

Molly sighed trying to check her impatience. She signaled Andre to press her harder and he nodded.

"So you went down and saw her body. But did you see who killed her?"

She turned away as if she hadn't heard the question and clucked her tongue a few more times until he patted her shoulder.

"I need to know, Checkers," he added emphatically. "This is very important. We're trying to find out who killed that little girl. I need your help."

"Just like when Briscoe and Green interview someone on TV?"

"Just like that. You're my witness. It's very important that you tell me what you know."

"It was the dark man. I was looking out the window. Laurie was on the swings. I wanted to call to her but I was too far away. He stood in front of her and was waving something. I know he frightened her. He frightened my Laurie!" Checkers clenched Andre's arm and stared into his eyes. "There was nothing I could do!"

"What happened next?"

"He faced her and then he shot her. She went down on the ground, and he walked away."

"Did you see where he went? Did he have a car?"

"I don't know. All I cared about was my Laurie. I should have saved her."

"Tell us about the man, Checkers," Molly interjected. "He was dark. Was he as dark as Andre?"

She shook her head. "No."

"What color was his hair?" Andre asked.

"Black."

"Hispanic," Molly whispered into his ear.

He nodded in agreement. "What was he wearing?"

She clucked her tongue repeatedly as she thought. "Sweatshirt and jeans, but there was something else… something I should tell you." She closed her eyes, trying to remember. She opened them and shook her head. "All I see is my Laurie and the blood."

"Are you sure?" he pressed.

She hung her head in disappointment. "I'm sorry, Detective Green."

They stood to go and he groaned, turning up his shoe. He'd stepped in gum. "I hate it when people are so inconsiderate."

He sat down again and Checkers suddenly grabbed his arm. "Detective Green, that's it! It was his shoes!"

After watching Checkers flip through five books of mug shots Molly doubted the old woman's ability to recall anything. She'd put together a vague headshot of the killer with the sketch artist, but there were no distinguishing features. Molly suspected it wouldn't do any good to circulate the picture. Still she seemed determined to study every potential face, but she hadn't spotted the man that she was sure she would recognize again.

"It was his shoes," she'd said over and over. "That's what was different. He was wearing jeans and a sweatshirt, but he had fancy black shoes on. Who wears fancy shoes with an old sweatshirt? And he had a metal necklace, but there was something wrong with it…"

As Checkers passed more pages without a reaction, Molly returned to the shoes. He was out of place. He didn't belong. She motioned to Andre and they stepped around the corner.

"What if Hector Cervantes hired a hit man?"

He looked skeptical. "Why would he do that? He's got a ton

of gang members who would do his bidding. Why would he pay someone? That doesn't make any sense."

"It would if he didn't want it to be connected to him. All the local boys are easily recognizable. It needed to look like a random killing by a stranger."

"No offense, Mol, but it sounds like a huge inconvenience to kill a little girl."

"Maybe an inconvenience but possibly necessary. He has a beef with Franco Perez and decides to take out Maria as a revenge killing, but he doesn't want to start an all out gang war so he hires someone. It'd be very hard to tie him to it. Think about the shoes. If he was a local guy why would he be wearing black dress shoes? He probably tried to dress the part, and he got out of town right after he left the schoolyard."

Andre pondered the idea and nodded. "I suppose it's possible."

"Franco Perez followed me yesterday," she said.

"Really?"

"He made it clear that if he finds out that Hector is connected to this, he's going to personally deal with it."

He closed his eyes obviously thinking of the consequences of a gang war. "That's about as bad as it gets."

They returned to Checkers' side as she closed the last book and clapped her hands together. "What else you got?"

Molly smiled at the twinkle in her eyes. She was a likeable character, and Molly couldn't help but wonder about her story and the daughter she claimed to have. Checkers had shed her trademark plaid jacket in the heated building. Molly saw that underneath was a sweatshirt with a cartoon cactus. No doubt a sympathetic vendor had given it to her. She was absolutely charming. Nearby was her bulging knapsack and Molly could only imagine the variety of objects that defined her existence.

"Checkers, are you sure the man was wearing black leather shoes?" Andre asked.

"Absolutely positive. He had a grey sweatshirt, blue jeans and those black shoes."

Suddenly she reached into her knapsack and removed a worn piece of paper. She glanced at the clock and checked the paper again before asking Molly, "Do you guys have a TV? It's almost time for my Laurie to come on."

Molly remembered what Bruce the security guard had mentioned. Checkers thought her daughter was a TV personality. She grabbed her remote and pointed it toward the tiny set that perched on her filing cabinet. Checkers was immediately engrossed as the music for the midday newscast began.

When Andre set four mug shots in front of her, she pushed them away.

"Not right now, Detective Green. I want to wait until a commercial."

They waited patiently until a car commercial popped up. He handed her four digital printouts that he'd downloaded from the FBI database that matched her sketch.

"Do you recognize any of these men?"

Checkers squinted at the grainy prints and studied each face carefully. "It's hard to tell." She sifted through them slowly, pausing briefly at one before quickly going through the other three. "It might be him."

She handed him the first photo and turned back to the set, the commercial break over. Molly compared the information attached to the photo. She'd identified Juan Benjarano, a known hired gun. His past hits involved shooting or strangling his victims—with a pocket chain.

"Checkers, didn't you say he had a chain?"

She chewed on her lip, thinking. "Yes, but it wasn't around his neck."

"Was it attached to his waist? Did it make a loop down his leg?"

She clapped her hands and smiled. "That's it!"

Molly sighed, realizing that there was little hope of finding Benjarano quickly. David Ruskin wouldn't be happy, but since she wasn't supposed to be in the precinct, he'd have to wait to get the news. She glanced at her watch. It was nearly twelve-thirty, and her head was spinning. She desperately craved a drink.

"Checkers, I need to take you to the shelter."

She wouldn't move from the screen. Molly noticed the knapsack by the table, its main pocket slightly opened. She reached down and casually sifted through the many papers, bus transfer slips and odds and ends inside. She unzipped the side pockets to discover gum, nuts and some fruit snacks. Looking closely in one of the interior pockets she spied a flap that led to a hidden compartment. She reached into it and extracted a very old pill bottle filled with mints. Most of the typewritten ink had faded and she could barely make out the date—June sixth, nineteen seventy-two. Originally the bottle had contained benzodiazepine. The patient's name was Millicent Jeffries. She looked up at the screen in disbelief as Laurel Jeffries signed off for the afternoon.

CHAPTER EIGHTEEN

Ari glanced at the clock on the 4Runner's dash unable to believe that most of the afternoon was gone. After visiting Stan Wertz she'd spent the day in the east valley previewing houses for a nice young couple looking to start a family. Ten houses later she found herself on the outskirts of Queen Creek, the most southern suburb of Phoenix.

She pulled into a Sonic and ordered a chili dog with fries. She'd skipped lunch, and the craving for junk food was overwhelming. Perhaps she was rebelling against all of the salads, tofu and whole grains she'd ingested for the past four months. When she took a bite of the unnatural and totally processed concoction, it felt like heaven in her mouth. Why had she shunned the foods she loved? *It's because of the heartburn and your ulcer.* But it was also an attempt to motivate Molly away from her beloved scotch.

She was drinking more and doing it secretly. Jane had heard that she was often parked on her favorite stool at Hideaway, and while she no longer picked up women, she drank—a lot. Given their fight this morning, Ari imagined that she was either at the bar right now or would be shortly. And perhaps to spite her, she'd claim some stranger for a one-night stand. She'd tried repeatedly to call her unable to shake the memory of waking up to her contorted, beet-red face and the aching bruise on her shoulder from the powerful shove.

But Molly hadn't picked up or answered her voice mail. Ari knew she shouldn't be surprised. The minute she'd agreed to represent Biz she'd guaranteed a confrontation with Molly, one that had more fireworks than the Fourth of July.

So why did she do it? She loved Molly. She didn't want to hurt her. Did she resent her jealousy? Was she attracted to Biz? She knew it wasn't the money, but that was the easy excuse she'd given Molly, who didn't believe it. She definitely enjoyed a comfortable lifestyle, and she was set thanks to some great advice from her old friend Bob, a financial advisor. It was because of him that she and Molly had met.

She popped the end of the chili dog into her mouth and opened her cell phone. She didn't want to be alone tonight, sitting in her condo and thinking of Molly with another woman. Maybe if that's what it took to get over her jealousy about Biz…

She dialed Jane and her father, who both agreed to a late dinner. Feeling better she pulled out of the Sonic, realizing that she was only a few blocks from the corner of Elliott and Alma School, the site of Stan Wertz's future megastore. As she approached the intersection she looked for an empty plot of land, but each corner housed active businesses. Confused, she pulled into a busy QuikTrip gas station on her right and studied the area. The QuikTrip was apparently new judging from the shiny exterior and fresh blacktop.

She scanned the three other corners, eyeing a medium-sized office building, an L-shaped strip mall and an old Victorian home that had obviously been rezoned for commercial purposes. She couldn't read the sign that sat close to the corner. It was as though the intersection had been designed decades ago with the

Victorian in mind. While the plot of land was rather large, she doubted a huge box store could fit in the space.

She shuddered at the notion of a bulldozer chewing away the beautiful front porch and wondered if she'd made a mistake. She closed her eyes and thought of Wertz's model. Was she right about the cross streets? Which corner was the right one? Had she confused the names? There was also an Ellsworth Road about ten miles east, but it ran parallel to Alma School.

She studied each corner carefully and dismissed the QuikTrip corner and the one to the south, the office building. It was at least five stories high and constructed in red brick. Whoever owned it wouldn't tear it down. She'd learned enough about commercial real estate from Lorraine to know that well-constructed office buildings lasted for decades. They might struggle during hard economic times, but they inevitably bounced back if they had the right location and this was certainly a prime one.

She decided to investigate the strip mall first since it would be the easiest to access. A quick maneuverg at the light and she was cruising along the storefronts. Several were empty and property management signs haphazardly hung in the windows. A few businesses were open—Daisy's Nail Salon, Only Batteries, Al's Furniture Depot and a dollar store that clearly wasn't part of a chain. Certainly not a thriving shopping center, but there were established businesses present.

"Let's just see what we can learn," she said.

She pulled into a parking space in front of the nail salon thinking about the chatty nail ladies she'd encountered whenever Jane dragged her in for a mani-pedi. The woman at the reception desk busily buffed her nails while another technician pampered an obviously desperate housewife who looked like she'd escaped her kids for a few hours while they were in school.

"May I help you?" the receptionist asked. "Manicure?"

Ari heard the hope in her voice. She batted her enormous false eyelashes and Ari was instantly turned off. She liked women who wore a minimal amount of makeup.

"Um, I actually wanted to ask you a weird question."

"Oh," the woman said and her shoulders sank. Business was definitely slow. "What do you need to know?"

"Is your strip mall being torn down?"

The nail technician's eyes jumped from the housewife to Ari in a second. She joined them at the counter. "Excuse me? Why are you asking that? Did that company send you here?"

Ari shook her head quickly, surprised. "Uh, no, I just wondered. This is a great location."

The woman eyed her suspiciously. "It's a great location and business will pick up soon. So if you're not here to support our business I suggest you leave."

"Um, okay," Ari said, backing out the door. *What the hell was that about?*

She pulled back onto Elliott and cruised through the intersection making an immediate left into the Victorian's parking lot. She could finally see the sign clearly—Drachman's Fine Smokes. It was a cigar store that closed at four. She'd have to come back.

She leaned against the 4Runner and sighed. Either she'd remembered the wrong streets or something was amiss. If this was the right intersection, one of these corners was going to be redone, but which one? And when? Wertz's model was complete. He wouldn't have commissioned an entire design for a place he wasn't ready to build, and there were laws about tenant notification.

She needed to see that model again, but she had no good excuse to visit him at his office. Her phone chirped, and she retreated inside the 4Runner to escape the traffic noise.

"Ari Adams."

"Ari, this is Biz. I thought I'd give you an update."

She laughed. "I'm the real estate agent. Shouldn't I be the one to give the updates?"

"Well, I do tend to take charge. I've already had my architect over at the loft, and she's optimistic that it will be easy to make the changes to the kitchen. So I'm ready to sign the papers. When can we meet?"

"I think it'll need to be tomorrow. I'm having dinner with Jane and my father tonight."

"Great. Tell Jane I said hello. Tell her that I approve of her latest girlfriend. That woman is *hot*."

Ari frowned. "And where did you meet this person?"

"At Hideaway. We literally ran into each other in the back room. Neither of us was paying attention to where we were going. We were, both, uh, concentrating on other things."

She closed her eyes. "That's way too much information," she said, annoyed. "Why don't I come by your office in the morning with the paperwork?"

"Huh. My keen detective abilities sense a bit of jealousy. Are you jealous, Ari?"

The humor in Biz's voice was evident, but Ari didn't want to play along. "Hardly."

"I've upset you," Biz correctly concluded. "I didn't mean to. I'm sorry for bringing up my sexual exploits, and if my flirting bothers you then I'm sorry twice." She sighed heavily over the phone. "It's just that I can't help it. I want you to be jealous and I *want* to flirt with you."

"You can't, Biz."

Another heavy sigh. "I know. The last thing I want to do is piss off Molly especially when she's in the middle of a gang shooting."

"What are you talking about? Is Maria Perez's murder gang related? That hasn't been reported."

"They only mentioned it in today's paper briefly but they've kept it quiet. My sources in the department are telling me that she was the brother of a gang lord, and it's a possible angle."

Her mind swirled with concern over Molly's safety. Gang members had no respect for the police. When she'd attended the police academy, she'd worked with the gang unit for a short time, learning the procedures and potential dangers of investigating gang shootings.

"Ari, are you still there?"

"I'm sorry, Biz. You've just surprised me. I didn't know. Look, I'll come to your office in the morning, and we'll take care of this paperwork. You'll have your loft by noon, okay?"

"Great. Again, I'm sorry. Can I make it up to you somehow?"

A thought came to her. "Actually how hard would it be for you to do a background check for me on Warren Edgington?"

"You're kidding, right?"

"What do you mean?"

"I've been hired by Edgington's wife, Christina. She doesn't believe he killed himself. She thinks he was murdered."

Ari headed up Rural Road to Jane's condo pondering Edgington's death and the fight he'd had with Stan Wertz right before he died. There was something fishy about her client, and her gut told her that he had something to do with Edgington's death.

She debated whether or not to call Molly, but she realized she had no concrete proof and more than likely her suspicion was baseless, grounded only in her supreme dislike for her client. And she imagined it would be another day at least before Molly would speak to her again. She could call Biz back, but there was something about her that made her nervous. She didn't know why every time she thought of the P.I., her hands started to sweat.

No, the person to talk to was Jane.

A silver Benz sat in Jane's driveway and she wondered if Jane had traded in her Porsche. When Jane didn't answer the doorbell, she called on her cell. Just as she was about to hang up Jane threw open the front door, her phone pressed against her ear.

"What?" she barked.

She noticed Jane wore only a slinky silk robe that barely covered the tops of her thighs. "I'm sorry," she stammered. "I didn't know you were busy."

"I'm entertaining," Jane whispered into the phone.

Ari giggled. "Why are we still talking on the phone when we're standing in front of each other?"

Jane flipped her phone closed and dropped it into the pocket of the robe. "You're early."

Ari checked her watch. "Only by ten minutes."

Jane sighed. "Ten minutes can make all the difference."

"Am I interrupting?" she asked.

"No, I was being facetious. That's my word of the day," Jane said with a grin. "Besides, we've already done it five times, and Laurel has to get to work."

Her eyes widened at Jane's announcement. "I'm shocked."

"What?" Jane responded. "Five's my average. It's no big deal."

"No, but screwing your client is." She immediately thought of Wertz propositioning her. "I thought you didn't like Laurel Jeffries."

Jane's blood red fingernails traced the neckline of her robe. "We've had a meeting of the minds. I found her the cutest little bungalow in the Willow area, and she was so overjoyed that she gave me a choice—a day at the spa or her. Guess what I picked?" A wicked smile crossed Jane's face as her eyes glanced up the staircase.

Ari turned to see Laurel descend, dressed in a gray suit, the smile of a news anchor plastered on her face. After a quick wink in Ari's direction, she went to Jane for a passionate kiss, her right hand slipping under the sheer fabric and roughly groping Jane's breast.

"Will I see you later tonight?" Laurel murmured into her mouth.

"Absolutely," Jane said before their tongues collided again.

Ari excused herself into Jane's kitchen, rather sure that there would be at least one more coupling in the foyer before Laurel left. She poured herself a glass of wine and picked up the newspaper, noticing that the Maria Perez murder was the headline of the local section. She instantly thought of Molly and the pressure she must be under. She buried herself in the article, trying to block out the moans emanating from the living room. Laurel would definitely be late.

The front door slammed shut, and Jane appeared in the kitchen, her face flushed and her cheeks rosy. "That was a wonderful way to end the afternoon," she proclaimed.

Ari set the newspaper down and stared at her friend. "I thought you'd made a few new rules, one being a clear division between clients and lovers?"

Jane shrugged her shoulders and made herself a vodka and tonic. "The line was clearly divided. We didn't go to bed until *after* I got her a house. Now, that's not to say that there wasn't some heavy petting and nudity in her new kitchen."

She shook her head in amazement. "Are you serious about Laurel?"

Jane delicately brought the patterned glass to her lips and sipped her drink. She set it down carefully before responding. "Honey, the word *serious* is right up there with commitment and relationship. We both know those are not words in my vocabulary, and thankfully Laurel has the same set of beliefs as I do." She looked up and beamed. "We are perfect for each other, aren't we?" Ari laughed and Jane squeezed her hand. "Enough about me for a while. Didn't you say you needed my help?"

"I do. But you're probably not going to like it. We could get into some trouble."

Her eyes twinkled, and she arched her eyebrows. "Really? Does it involve danger?"

"I doubt it. But it does involve a woman in an incredibly sexy pink bra."

Jane jumped off her stool and charged back up the stairs. She rejoined her in three minutes dressed in a tight pantsuit with very low cleavage.

"Let's go. I'll do most anything for a woman in a pink bra."

Ari worked her way downtown, driving against the rush hour traffic. She'd called his office, confirming with the very polite receptionist that Mr. Wertz was indeed gone for the day, but Candy was still available and could certainly help Ms. Adams with her missing files. She recounted her suspicions about Wertz to Jane, including her encounter with him at the preview house.

"He really asked you to unbutton your blouse?" Jane asked in disbelief.

"Yes. He's really slimy, but he's worth a lot of money."

Jane buffed her French nails and checked the shine. "Then he's worth it. Period. You'll deal with it unless he's a killer," she quickly added. "In that case, I'd ask for a double commission."

"Jane!"

Ari pulled into the parking garage for the second time that day. They strolled through the cavernous lobby, all of the business people cruising home except for Candy, who she suspected was a workaholic and devoted to her boss.

"You know what to do, right?" she asked as they boarded the elevator.

Jane sighed. "Ari, honey, you've got nothing to worry about. Take your time. I've got it covered. You're dealing with a professional."

She followed Jane down the long corridor to Candy's desk, well aware that her swinging hips were sure to gain the attention of the secretary with the pink bra. When they reached the outer lobby, Candy was engrossed in her typing and unaware of their initial approach until Jane's perfume wafted through the air. She turned to find her leaning over her desk, exposing most of her cleavage.

"Hi, I'm Jane, Ari's friend. You remember Ari, don't you?" Jane motioned to her and she smiled.

"Of course. Hello, Ari. Hello, Jane." She stared at Jane, whose breasts sprawled over much of her desk demanding attention. She leaned forward as Jane whispered to her. She giggled in response, and Ari knew it was time to make her move.

"If it's all right with you, Candy, I'm just going to slip into Stan's office and get those files. That's okay, isn't it?"

"Sure," Candy replied with a laugh. Jane smiled and let her index finger trail down the side of Candy's cheek.

Ari disappeared into the office and went straight to the model. Her eyes focused on the intersection and the chosen location—the corner with the L-shaped strip mall. She studied the mini-version of Wertz's dream carefully. It was a typical big box type store, one that would never have a secondary use if the Hometown City Center failed. A spec list sat next to the model, listing the square footage, amenities and projected date of completion—Christmas. She shook her head unable to believe that in less than ten months the entire corner would be transformed.

How could that be? The tenants didn't even know they were losing their shops. There was something illegal about his deal. She grabbed her cell phone and snapped a few pictures of the model and the spec sheet.

She went to his desk and computer. His screensaver flashed neon colors and the Hometown logo. As she suspected he relied entirely on Candy, not even bothering to shut down his computer or lock his desk. She rifled through his drawers, not knowing what to look for and finding nothing but standard office supply items—and a vibrator. She was sure she knew who played with Stan and his little toy. She tapped on the mouse and the screen filled with his desktop icons, none of which looked suspicious. She clicked on his document folder and was told to enter a password. His E-mail was also protected and she didn't have time to try to figure it out.

She clicked on his personal calendar and scrolled backward looking for anything that suggested a connection to Warren Edgington. She hoped for a specific reference such as *Meet Warren and kill him*, but there were no entries that mentioned him or the Hometown City Center property. A thud reverberated under her feet and she froze. She looked at the door, expecting Candy to burst into the room, but no one entered. Everything else in the office was in place except for a strange modern print that hung slightly askew as if someone had moved it recently. She pulled the painting from the wall to discover a safe. She halfheartedly flipped the metal handle certain that the lock was engaged. Her hunch was correct and the door didn't budge.

She quickly replaced the painting and opened the office door slowly. Jane and Candy had disappeared but she found the source of the thud—a large crystal paperweight lay on its side in front of Candy's desk making a deep impression in the plush carpet. She searched through the files and stacks of correspondence next to her computer and the pile of papers in her inbox. It seemed Wertz participated in every decision and micromanaged each of his stores.

She quickly scanned the desktop amongst the knickknacks and personal photos. A few memos with sticky notes awaited her attention, but they contained typical information about meat sales and freezers. There was no way to tell what was important.

Candy's screensaver materialized—a picture of a convertible BMW. And how could she afford that? Perhaps it was just a dream or maybe a Beemer was Wertz's way of buying her silence.

She checked Candy's calendar which was incredibly organized. Her handwriting was impeccable and she annotated many of the entries with sticky notes, receipts or follow-up phone messages. Ari cracked a grin. She and Candy could be great friends.

She flipped back to Monday and her heart stopped. Candy had crossed out all of Monday afternoon and written *Dr. Murris*. There were no other notes, but she'd obviously expected to be gone for several hours—and wouldn't know whether Stan had returned to the office at one o'clock as he'd told the police.

She flipped back a few more days, the sticky notes fluttering with each turn of the page. She'd reviewed nearly two weeks when a name on a receipt caught her eye, Drachman's Fine Smokes. The notes indicated Candy had left early one afternoon and gone to the Smoke Shop to make a purchase. The receipt only listed a number and the price, thirty-five dollars.

She threw open the lid of Candy's desktop copier and stuck the receipt on the glass. She heard laughter—Jane's cue. Once the machine had spit out a copy of the receipt, Ari flipped Candy's book to February first and copied the evidence that proved her absence.

Jane's shrill laughter exploded into the room, and Ari heard a door open behind her. She quickly returned Candy's book to her desk, grabbed an empty file folder and dropped onto the couch. She hoped she didn't look totally out of breath as she stood to greet a smiling Candy and Jane, whose tongue was fastened to her earlobe.

"Now, baby, c'mon," Candy coaxed. "Not in front of Ari. Did you find your folders?" Candy asked.

"Oh, yes. Thanks."

Candy nodded and returned to her desk, her hand caressing Jane's buttocks as she swept by.

"Thanks again, Candy. We need to go, Jane."

Ari reached the elevators and waited for the car to arrive. When the doors slid open, Jane still had not appeared. She held the door for almost a minute before Jane marched down the hallway, Candy watching her departure from her desk.

"I hope you got what you needed," Jane said. "That woman was an animal."

"I'm sorry it was so painful," she cracked. She pulled the copies from her pocket and showed them to her.

"So maybe Candy killed her lover," Jane said. "Wertz thinks she's at the doctor's and she's really over in the garage using the flask she bought. Or she lied for her boss and he did it."

"Or nobody did it and he really committed suicide," Ari said with a sigh. She watched the blinking red numbers count down to the ground floor. "It's probably nothing. I'm sorry I dragged you down here for nothing."

"Nothing?" Jane snorted. "I had a much better time than you did."

"I take it you saw the pink bra?"

In one quick gesture she pulled the bra from her purse, and waved it under her nose.

CHAPTER NINETEEN

Molly was sure it was over. Ari had called repeatedly but never left a message. She remembered the look on her face during her drunken rage that morning. It was fear. She'd never let the box of jealousy fly open in Ari's presence. She kept everything buried and only revealed what she wanted Ari to see—until now.

"Here," Vicky said, dropping a scotch in front of her.

She shook her head. She wasn't going to get stopped again. "No, I'm done. Bring me some coffee."

"You sure you want to turn down a free drink from a beautiful lady?"

Vicky motioned to an attractive blonde on the other side of the bar. Their eyes met and the blonde held up her shooter in salute and downed it, thrusting her significant cleavage out in the process. She slapped the shot glass down on the bar and smiled at her.

She smiled and sipped her drink. One more wouldn't hurt.

The blonde left her stool and dropped next to her. "You look like you could use a little something."

"Thanks for the drink. That was nice of you."

"You're welcome," she said, and Molly could hear the thickness of her speech. "I'm on my last one. I've had a hell of a week, but after I finish this I'm going home."

Molly pointed at the empty shot glass in front of her. "I guess you've already finished."

The blonde eyed the shooter and laughed heartily. Her breath stank of tequila and Molly imagined she was way over the legal limit. There was no way she could drive.

"How are you getting home?" Molly asked.

A depraved smile crept across her face. "Are you tryin' to pick me up?"

She shook her head. "No, I've got a girlfriend. I just don't think you should drive. Is there someone you could call?"

The woman shook her finger as if to make a point. "Now see, that's the problem. I just broke up with the one person I could call. Isn't that always how it goes? You break up and find yourself in a bar and the person you'd call is the reason you're there in the first place."

Molly chuckled. She was right. The woman was a natural beauty and her impulses stirred. She couldn't help it. She bit her lip to remind herself that she was faithful to Ari. They sat in silence, stealing glances at each other.

"What's your name?" Molly finally asked.

"Lola," the woman replied, grinning in a way that told Molly she was lying. "And you're Molly, the cop."

"How'd you know?"

"I asked." She nodded at Vicky. "And I'd like you to drive me home," she added, in a suggestive tone.

So there it was, an opportunity. She could pour out her frustrations with a stranger and fill the void in her heart that Ari created. Lola's long fingernails trailed down her thigh intensifying the heat between her legs.

"I couldn't drive you home right now," she croaked, practically unintelligibly. "I'm not sober myself."

Lola's cool expression read between the lines. "And what sort of citizen would I be if I didn't help a member of the law enforcement community?"

Her nails pressed against Molly's pants, leaving scratch marks on the fabric. She could only imagine what her thighs looked like, and she hoped she wasn't bleeding. After her lecture to Ari about Biz, the last thing she needed was to be clawed like an animal.

Molly grasped her hand but didn't let go. She needed to let go. She knew that. But the image of Biz's name on the file folder, written in Ari's careful, meticulous script, wouldn't allow her to release the soft hand she now held.

"Come with me," Lola said, sliding off the stool and heading for the back room.

She followed, her gaze darting around the bar until she was certain that Jane wasn't there. They found a plush sofa in a dark corner. Lola pressed against her, and Molly inhaled her scent, so different from Ari's. Lola wore heavy cologne that smelled like a bouquet of flowers, and her lips ravaged Molly's neck, smothering her willpower.

She closed her eyes as Lola unbuttoned her shirt, exposing her flesh to the cool air conditioning of the back room. The purple nails wandered across the hills of her breasts, and she threw her eyes open in panic, picturing deep scratches that she couldn't hide from Ari.

Lola grinned, obviously reading her mind. "Do you know why I keep my nails so long?"

"No," Molly whispered.

"Because I never use my hands. That's what my tongue's for."

Her eyes widened at the surprising response. She was too stunned to move and did nothing when Lola climbed on top of her and began rocking her hips.

"C'mon, Detective, let's get to third base. Then you can drive me home."

CHAPTER TWENTY

Ari yawned repeatedly as she headed for Biz's office. She should've known that dinner with her father and Jane would be a five-hour affair, ending with a quick trip to the Ak-Chin Casino and Jack's favorite game—blackjack. While he and Jane amassed a small fortune, she continually slipped outside and tried to reach Molly who never answered.

She returned her attention to Biz's address and pulled into a small parking lot in front of a quaint old building. Her office was part of a converted farmhouse which included several businesses under one roof. She parked her SUV next to Biz's Mustang and entered through the main door. A maze of hallways tunneled through the house. She only made one wrong turn before she found the door with a simple gold placard announcing, *Elizabeth Stone, Private Investigator.*

She opened the door to find Biz and a young woman in the midst of a passionate kiss. They quickly broke apart at the sight of her, the young woman blushing and reaching for her purse. She bolted out of the room as Ari offered an apology, but the woman's face remained downward, unwilling to look at her.

When the door quickly slammed shut she turned to Biz. "I'm sorry. I *do* know how to knock."

Biz smiled and shrugged, unembarrassed. "Not a big deal. That was Callie. She was just delivering my lunch." She picked up a brown bag, the name of a local deli emblazoned across the side.

"Is that your girlfriend?"

"No."

She raised a cynical eyebrow. "Really? That was quite a kiss."

Biz motioned for her to sit on the couch and dropped into an old wooden chair, propping her cowboy boots up on the desk. "Thanks for the compliment, but that was just a fortunate moment."

Her office had few furnishings—her desk, a filing cabinet, a back table stacked with papers and the couch Ari sat upon. No pictures or art adorned the tan walls, only a printed piece of paper that she'd tacked above her desk. It read simply, *It is what it is, you get what you get, and whatever happens, happens.*

"It's good to see you," she said cheerfully.

"I'm glad to see you, too," Ari said. She so enjoyed her genuine friendliness. It was unusual and refreshing. "I've brought the contract, which is really a formality since you're not negotiating the price and you're dealing with a company."

She moved from the clunky office chair to the sofa next to her. She listened attentively as Ari explained the details, and unlike many of her clients who merely nodded during her standard contract spiel, she asked several questions about the passages and clauses, often testing her broader knowledge of several topics. By the time she was ready to sign she'd given Ari a professional workout.

"There. It's done," Biz pronounced, holding out the pen and contract to her.

"Do you feel any different?"

"Poorer," Biz laughed. "But this place is home, you know? I'm sure I won't regret it."

A touch of jealousy pulled at her heart. She had yet to really find a home. She double-checked the contract while she chatted with Biz. "I'm glad you feel that way. It's tough dealing with clients who get a large dose of buyer's remorse. When I turn this contract in to the company, it's binding."

Biz waved her hand unfazed by the commitment or the legal obligation. "That won't happen. In fact if you've got the time, I'll go down there with you right now and turn it in, and I can show you what my contractor is going to do to the kitchen. How about it? Then I'll take you to lunch."

"What about your lunch from Callie?" Ari asked, motioning to the bag. "Won't she be disappointed if you don't eat it?"

Biz slowly turned her head and concentrated on her expression. "I'm not particularly worried about Callie's feelings. I'd rather have lunch with you."

She swallowed hard. "I can't. I'm meeting my father for lunch. But I promise I'll get the contract in today."

Biz accepted the rejection with a nod. "Ari, I have a question for you. Are you and Molly a couple?"

"Of course. We've been together for several months. Why do you ask?"

Biz stared at the floor. "It's just that…"

"What?"

There was a sharp edge to her voice that came out accidentally. When Biz looked up seriously, she knew what she was going to say. Molly hadn't returned any of her phone calls the night before and when she'd finally called Andre in a flurry of paranoia and concern, he'd hesitantly confirmed that she'd left before six. She knew where she'd gone and so did Biz.

Biz sighed. "It's nothing." She shifted on the sofa. "Hey, when I called you yesterday why did you ask me about Edgington?"

"I was just curious."

She flashed a knowing smile and leaned back on the sofa. "I'm not going to believe that so why don't you tell me the truth?"

She gazed into her eyes, lost in the fascinating gold flecks. "I hardly know you."

"But you can trust me," she whispered.

Her voice was almost hypnotic, and her eyes didn't lie. Ari immediately understood why so many women sought her help. It was her sincerity and definitely her eyes. She swallowed hard and leaned back on the sofa. "If Warren Edgington's wife is correct about him being murdered then I think one of my clients or his secretary are prime suspects."

Biz listened carefully as Ari outlined her suspicions, including the fight at the luncheon, Edgington's affair with Candy and the mysterious Hometown Center location.

"Everything you've got is entirely circumstantial," Biz said.

"You're probably right. I just think the whole thing is really coincidental. I saw them arguing and then Edgington winds up dead. Wertz's secretary provided an alibi, but she wasn't at the office. I looked up the doctor she visited. Biz, he works for Planned Parenthood. I'm rather certain that Candy went to get an abortion."

"You said Candy and Edgington were lovers. Do you think it was his baby?"

"Maybe," Ari said, "or it was Wertz's. I'm rather certain they've hooked up."

Biz rubbed her chin. "None of this makes any sense, but I'll do some digging."

"No," Ari disagreed. "I need to know whether my client is a murderer. You can help me, but I'm looking into this myself."

Biz smiled seductively. "So if I agree to help you, does that mean you and I can spend the afternoon together?

Biz insisted on driving. With her hand slung out the open window, cigarette in hand, and her dark shades a perfect match for her black outfit and hair, she truly looked dangerous—and very appealing.

"What?" Biz asked, her eyes on the road.

"What do you mean, *what*?"

"You're staring at me, Ari. Do I have some sort of disgusting thing coming out of my nose or are you debating whether or not monogamy with your girlfriend is a good thing?"

"You're pretty sure of yourself, aren't you?"

"Well, I'm really hoping that a booger isn't dangling out of my nostril."

"Gross!" she laughed.

Biz flashed a megawatt smile, punched a button on the dash and filled the car with Katy Perry's latest song. Ari leaned back and ran her fingers through her hair. Her life was in chaos, and everything was out of place. Her relationship with Molly was in shambles, her father wanted to start over and her most prominent client could possibly be a murderer. She glanced through the window at the cars speeding by, refusing to focus on any details. Maybe it would all work out. Ironically it was her father who proved to be the most reasonable person. He'd accepted her lunch cancellation graciously. He was really trying which was more than she could say for Molly, who wouldn't return her calls. She was either still royally pissed about Biz or she was ashamed because she'd had a one-night stand.

Biz exited the 101 and they cruised down Elliott to Alma School. "Let's hit the strip mall first."

Instead of driving around the front Biz went behind the stores, slowing the car to a crawl. It looked quite standard to Ari. Each business had a back entrance. The furniture store was equipped with a large loading bay that was presently being used by three delivery men loading up their truck. Biz stopped ten feet away and they watched various sofas and loveseats disappear inside.

"That's odd," Biz said.

"What do you mean?"

"They're only loading couches and sofas."

Ari shrugged. "Maybe that's all anyone's bought. Maybe they're having some sort of sale."

Biz leaned forward against the steering wheel. "But what are the chances of that happening? If you go to a furniture store, isn't it likely that you'd buy at least one other item? Maybe a lamp or a coffee table? There's more furniture in a living room than the couch."

They continued to watch the transfer of furniture as more sofas made their way onto the truck. Biz was right.

"Where do you think they're taking all of it?" Ari finally asked. "It looks like they've emptied out the whole department."

"It seems that way," Biz agreed. She put the car into drive, and they continued to cruise behind the strip mall. "Wait a sec," she said, stopping the car suddenly.

She headed to the back door of a vacant store, leaning over to read the property manager's sign. Ari followed and scanned the fine print. The property management company was Cardiff industries, a division of EPI.

"What's EPI?" she asked Biz, sensing it must be important.

She cracked a grin. "EPI stands for Edgington Properties International. Cardiff is a subdivision of Warren Edgington's parent corporation."

"That can't be a coincidence," Ari said.

She nodded. "I think we've learned what we need to know."

"Which is?"

Biz crossed her arms and glanced back at the truck now rumbling away. "There was some sort of deal between Edgington and your guy, Stan Wertz—"

"Please don't call him *my* guy."

She laughed. "Understood. Anyway, I think they made a deal on this property, but the only tenant who knows is the furniture store owner. He's got an inside track, and he's cleaning out."

"Why does he know and nobody else?"

"Hard to say. He's either moving to another location or to a storage facility. Either way it takes time." She took Ari's hand and squeezed. "It doesn't matter. Look, you need to be careful, okay? I don't know what's going on, but this connection between Edgington and Wertz…"

She didn't finish her sentence. Ari knew what she meant and nodded.

Biz pulled her close and whispered, "Be careful. I couldn't stand it if anything happened to you."

Ari ducked out of the embrace and headed for the car, certain that Biz wanted to kiss her. As they drove across the street to the Victorian house she wasn't sure how she felt about that.

When they entered the smoke shop her senses were assaulted by twenty odors hovering in the small lobby. The pungent smells of the stogies behind the glass case combined with the wafting smoke from the back parlor room where men enjoyed their recently purchased cigars reminded her of a barnyard. The look on her face must have telegraphed her obvious displeasure.

"Not a fan?" Biz asked.

"No. What about you?"

"I've smoked a few cigars in my time, but it's not my vice of choice."

No one had yet appeared to help them so they looked around at the displays, all of which were affiliated with smoking, drinking and gambling. Laughter erupted from the back room and she could hear the distinct baritones of men bonding together beyond the brown curtain. She made a mental note to remember this place as her father claimed all three activities for his favorite pastimes—after fishing. She pulled out the receipt and noticed the purchase was for thirty-five dollars so whatever Candy had bought for Wertz was somewhat expensive.

"May I help you?"

They turned to see a middle-aged Indian man dressed in a button-down shirt and sweater vest emerge from behind the curtain. His bushy mustache hid his mouth, and Ari wasn't sure if he'd actually spoken the words to them.

"Yes," Biz answered. "I was hoping you could help us. My uncle Fred made a purchase here about a week or so ago, and I don't know if you were the gentleman who helped him. Would there be someone else who works here, too?"

"I am Rudy. My brother is Natel."

Biz snapped her fingers in fake recognition. "Yup. I think that was him. Anyway, Uncle Fred bought something and got this receipt."

She handed the copied receipt to Rudy, who studied the purchase.

"No refunds," he barked and thrust the paper back at her.

"Oh, I'm not looking for a refund. See, Uncle Fred has dementia. He doesn't remember much. He can't remember what he bought, and I know this will sound ridiculous but my mom, his sister, keeps track of his money and the way he spends it. It's for the government and his social security. My mother would most appreciate it if you could perhaps tell us what he spent the money on in your store."

He narrowed his eyes, and Ari didn't know if he saw through Biz's story or if he believed that men were entitled to their secrets from womenfolk. Without giving him much time to think, Biz leaned over the counter and looked at the receipt. "He didn't spend it on cigars, did he?"

He shook his head. "No, they would ring up differently. He purchased a single item, but it could have been a variety of things, such as a pipe, a flask, even a solid pewter mug. There are many possibilities."

"Oh," Biz said dejectedly.

"I cannot help you anymore. I advise you to leave your poor uncle alone. If he has the Alzheimer's, you should let him enjoy the little pleasures that he can afford."

The phone rang and Rudy busied himself with a client, working the computer next to the cash register. Ari started for the door but Biz stopped her before she could open it. Rudy had his back to them, still on the phone. When he hung up he headed to his friends in the back room. Biz's eyes lingered on the bright computer screen.

"No," Ari cautioned, but Biz was already moving behind the counter, the receipt in her hand. She found the inventory icon and tapped the item number into the search. The computer slowly processed the request. Ari noticed the men's laughter had receded—they were talking as if they were preparing to leave.

"Biz, they're coming."

"I know, just a few more seconds." The computer made a slight groan before a beep signaled the information was retrieved.

They watched as the item name appeared on the screen. Candy had purchased a silver flask. The men's voices were right behind the fabric curtain and Ari quickly pulled her out from behind the counter. There was no time to escape. When Rudy emerged, leading his friends out of the back room, he came upon the two women, their lips locked in a steamy kiss.

"Oh, shit!" Rudy screamed. "Get out of my shop!"

CHAPTER TWENTY-ONE

The search for Juan Benjarano proved fruitless. Molly and Andre checked with countless law enforcement agencies and searched multiple databases with no luck. They even scoured the surveillance cameras at Sky Harbor Airport hoping to ascertain whether he'd hopped on a plane in the last few days.

"He's probably long gone," Andre said. "And I'm sure he had an escape route planned. He's a professional."

Molly could hear the frustration in his voice. She was tired and her head ached. She'd had one too many last night and hadn't slept at all, her mind filled with Ari and Lola. Ari was dangerous, uncharted territory, while Lola, a complete stranger, represented comfort and familiarity. *How ironic.*

They'd indeed gotten to third base in the back room. It was as far as they could legally go in a public place, and Molly had driven her home while she whispered all the delectable things she wanted to do with her when they got there. But she couldn't get out of the truck. Her fingers gripped the steering wheel and wouldn't let go even when Lola playfully tried to pry them off. She just shook her head until the passenger's door slammed shut and Lola disappeared.

She imagined Ari would call her a cheater and now she didn't know what to do. Andre had confessed that Ari had called and she'd grilled him until he admitted she wasn't at work. Ari was too smart not to know what had happened. And she was too ashamed to call her.

"Mol, I may have found something," Andre announced, pointing to her infamous spreadsheet and pulling her from her misery.

She noticed it was quite crinkled and covered in coffee stains. He'd highlighted various streets and marked up the margins with his notes as he searched each address.

"Remember how I told you I wanted to concentrate on those four addresses?"

She nodded. "What are you thinking?"

He pointed at two that were conveniently located on the same page. "These are interesting. The other two are dead ends. The limited corporations that are listed actually feed into larger corporations that may be involved in some questionable activity, but I'm highly doubtful that it connects to our situation. That leaves the other two."

He opened the spreadsheet and read his notes. "This one, Periscope Enterprises, is a front for a larger limited entity called Wayburn Incorporated. From what I can tell this is clearly a dummy front because they have absolutely no background or history. I've searched through a ton of websites and search engines and there's nothing. I even came in early and did a little digging on our police sites, and I can't find a mention. Very suspicious."

She raised an eyebrow. "That has possibilities. It also sounds like we wouldn't know what to do with it even if it was the right one."

"We don't have to know. We just go and stake out the address.

If it's related to the department I'm sure we'll be able to make a connection."

"You think we'll see someone we know."

He grinned. "Absolutely."

A load lifted from her shoulders. They might actually figure this out. She hated dirty cops, and she felt responsible for her informant's death. "What about the other one?"

He tapped the spreadsheet page. "This one also has promise. The listed owner is Rogue River Corporation and it's a subsidiary of a company called Duffek Turn. No such entity is registered with the Better Business Bureau or anyone else. I even called Oregon where the actual Rogue River is located and they have no corporation on record. It's a dummy."

She leaned forward, her nerves tingling. "So you think that if we stake out these two houses we may see the mole."

He shrugged. "I think it's worth a try."

She clapped her hands together unable to contain her excitement. "Okay, how about this weekend? Are you willing to help me out a little longer?"

"Sure, but you owe me a whole bunch of sandwiches from McGurkee's."

"I was thinking a steak dinner, but I'll go with the sandwiches. They're cheaper."

There was a knock on the door, and Jack Adams stuck his head inside. She bit her lip, hoping she could contain her emotions. Looking at him only reminded her of Ari.

"Hey, Detective Nelson," he said jovially. "I hope I'm not interrupting."

She waved him inside. "Not at all. Jack Adams, this is Andre Williams, my partner."

The men shook hands as Jack surveyed the room. When his eyes met hers, he grinned.

"You're probably wondering why I keep disturbing you and why I've been checking out your office."

She shrugged. "No, actually neither of those thoughts crossed my mind."

He laughed. "Well, I'm glad. I wouldn't want you to think I was some sort of leech. These were my digs a long time ago."

Her eyes widened. "Really?"

"Yup."

Ari had never mentioned that fact to her, and she wondered why. Maybe it was during the period of estrangement when Jack had disowned Ari and they weren't speaking.

"I just wanted to stop by and see how you were coming with the case. Any leads?"

He crossed his arms and she couldn't help but notice his incredibly broad shoulders. He was a huge man, and she imagined he intimidated suspects just with his presence.

"We're working on a few things, but it hasn't popped yet."

He nodded. His eyes traveled her desk and landed on the spreadsheet. "What's that?"

She shrugged, hoping she looked nonchalant. "Nothing, really. Unrelated to the case."

He eyed her suspiciously and said, "Well, if there's anything this retired guy can do to help you, let me know. I'm in town until tomorrow."

He left, and she immediately deposited the spreadsheet into her desk drawer. She wondered if he'd noticed the two addresses that Andre had circled. Her stomach flip-flopped at the realization that the Rogue River Corporation was named after a river in Oregon—Jack Adams's adopted state. She was so focused on her thoughts that she didn't bother to check the caller ID when her phone rang.

"Nelson."

"I'd like to have lunch. But only if you want to."

Ari's quiet voice was barely audible, and Molly covered her other ear to block out the incessant noise of the precinct.

A lump formed in her throat. Her hands began to shake. "Okay."

Ari had finished her second tumbler of iced tea by the time Molly finally appeared in the doorway of Chen's Chinese Kitchen, nearly thirty minutes late. She looked hung over, and her suit was wrinkled. *Probably the one she wore yesterday.* That wasn't a good sign.

Her gaze fell on Ari, offering a weak smile as she approached.

"Sorry I'm late," she apologized, squeezing her large frame into the booth. "We've had a lot going on, and I couldn't get away until David Ruskin had his pound of flesh."

"Some things never change," Ari said.

They glanced at each other and both started to speak at the same time. They abruptly stopped and looked away. The waitress came by and Ari wasn't surprised when Molly ordered a scotch. She kept her gaze downward, certain that if she looked at her, Molly would see reproof in her eyes, and another fight would begin.

After the waitress took their lunch order and disappeared, she cleared her throat and said, "I'm sorry I didn't tell you about Biz. I guess I just wanted to avoid the confrontation. I knew you'd be upset."

Molly bit her lip. Ari could tell she was trying to word her next statement carefully. "I just don't understand why you took her on as a client. Couldn't she have gone to Jane or Lorraine?"

"I suppose. But she trusts me the most."

Molly snorted. "Of course."

She stared at her. "Please don't go there. You trust *me*, don't you?"

Molly nodded, her eyes focused on the linen tablecloth. "I trust you, but I don't trust Biz. I've known her for a lot longer, and she isn't what she seems. She's not forthright—especially when it comes to women. She wants what she wants, and she'll do whatever she can to get it. She's got a mean streak, too."

Ari shook her head unable to fathom a dark side to Biz. Of course she knew Biz was a womanizer, and she wondered how a private investigator could have enough money to buy such expensive property but Biz seemed quite genuine.

"You don't have anything to worry about, honey. Believe me, okay? I love you, and I know how hard it is for you to say it. I know how hard it is for you to commit."

Molly shrugged, clearly unwilling to lie. "I'm sorry," she said.

Her drink appeared, and she drained the glass quickly, motioning to the departing waitress for another. Ari looked away, biting her tongue. She waited, hoping that Molly would apologize for her part of the fight, for shoving Ari and for whatever had transpired last night that forced her to wear a rumpled suit to work. Now would be the perfect time since she'd coated her emotions with a little alcohol, and there was nothing else to occupy their time. The food hadn't arrived and they were just sitting, listening to the humming restaurant.

"Is there something you'd like to tell me?"

Molly whipped her head toward Ari, whose eyes studied the rumpled suit. It was like receiving a telegram. Molly was a detective. She must realize that Ari knew what had happened. And she needed to say something, but she only offered a "thank you," when the waitress returned with her second drink.

Ari realized lunch was a mistake, but now she was stuck for the duration. Fortunately Chen's was known for their quick service. She could be back in her office in another forty minutes. *Just talk about work.*

"I heard your case might be gang related. Is that true?"

Molly sipped her drink. It was obvious to Ari she debated how much she should share. "We're not sure. It looks as though a hit man might have been hired, but we don't know why. It's so senseless. Who could kill a child?" she added in frustration.

She swirled her drink, and Ari knew the case was eating her up. She longed to reach across the table and take her hand or touch her arm, but she could still feel Molly's shove. A chill ran down her back just thinking about it.

"It's terrible," she simply said.

Molly nodded, her gaze never leaving the scotch. "Children are so innocent. Only a really sick person can kill a child. Even in prison there's a code against child molesters and killers. Most hardened criminals still have a soft spot for kids." She suddenly stopped talking and took a deep breath. "I would have preferred the Edgington case, frankly."

At the mention of Warren Edgington, Ari shifted in her seat. There was no way she could share anything with Molly right now as it would lead to a discussion of Biz, a woman whose kiss still lingered on her lips. After they'd fled the shop, Biz had laughed and teased her all the way back to her office, claiming she'd tongued her. Ari protested and soon was laughing herself. She compared sitting in Biz's Mustang with sitting in the booth waiting for lunch and found herself hoping Molly got an emergency call or text as she sometimes did.

She decided to make one more effort as the food arrived. "I told my dad that I was seeing someone in the department."

Molly raised an eyebrow. "Really?"

"Yeah. Maybe we could get together for lunch tomorrow before he leaves. Would that work?"

Molly expertly wielded her chopsticks through her chicken chow mien. "I'll have to see," she said. "Maybe."

"Let me know," she said quietly, pushing back the tears she knew could come so easily.

They ate in silence. Ari realized they'd never had a meal like this, not even their first date, when Molly had been terrified the whole evening. Yet it had still ended magnificently. She wondered if this wasn't a different kind of ending.

Her gaze wandered to the bar area and the TV perched above the patrons. Desperate for small talk she pointed to the screen when Laurel Jeffries came on.

"That's the woman Jane's dating right now."

Molly looked at her, surprised. "You're kidding. Really?"

She nodded. "She sold her a house and apparently much more."

Usually conversation about Jane would cause them to laugh, but Molly surprised her by saying, "I know her mother. She's my witness."

"What?"

She'd heard much of Laurel's biography during the past few weeks at Tuesday coffee and it didn't include a mother. Laurel had been raised by her father back East and then relatives after he died.

"She doesn't have a mother. Laurel said she's dead," Ari added.

Molly shook her head. "She isn't dead. She probably should get the award for worst parent. She abandoned her, at least that's what she says."

"What?"

"I don't know. She could barely talk about it, and the info could be all wrong. The woman has Alzheimer's and getting anything out of her has been a guessing game. She said Laurel Jeffries was her daughter."

"But you said she had Alzheimer's. Maybe she's just saying that because she sees her on TV."

"Possibly. But I know her name is Millicent Jeffries. Found it on a pill bottle in her possessions."

"Wow, that's really amazing," she said, forgetting her own problems for a moment.

She couldn't imagine what it would've been like to have her mother abandon her. How horrible it must've been for Laurel. Lucia had been a wonderful mother until the end.

Lost in her own thoughts of her mother, she didn't notice Molly checking her messages. When she looked up, Molly was standing, draining her scotch and tossing some bills on the table.

"I need to go," she said.

"I really—"

"Look, Ari, I'm not sure where we are. I'll call you later."

She stared into the crystal blue eyes she loved, remembering that someone else had met Molly's gaze the night before and shared her bed. She saw the pain that Molly was desperately trying to mask with alcohol, and she knew she'd caused it by spending time with Biz.

"Are you okay to drive?" she asked automatically, avoiding the question and shoving the pain away.

Molly's face softened. She nodded before she walked away.

CHAPTER TWENTY-TWO

Molly faced the sea of Valentine's Day cards in the Hallmark store while she worked to quell the panic that gripped her. Hundreds of hearts and stuffed animals mocked her all proclaiming the one sentiment that Ari longed to hear every day—I love you. And she'd learned to say it frequently. She'd even practiced saying it in front of the mirror to ensure her facial expressions and body language were believable.

After their horrible lunch she'd spent the afternoon thinking of Ari, her mistake with Lola and a way to make it right. Tomorrow was Valentine's Day—a perfect opportunity—but she was lost.

The store was filled with people like her who had procrastinated for the past month and now faced their lover's wrath if they missed the big day. She automatically flipped open her phone and hit her brother's speed dial number. If anyone knew anything about romance it was Brian.

"I guess Lynn owes me a foot massage," he said in place of a greeting. Lynn was Brian's long-time girlfriend.

"Why?"

"Because I bet her that you would call me before Valentine's Day, asking for my advice."

"She gives me way too much credit," she said. "I guess I should thank you for keeping my phobias and anxieties a secret."

"You're welcome. Now, where are you? Jewelry or card store?"

She groaned. "Card store. It's like the Good Ship Lollypop exploded everywhere. I can't deal with all this sugary sweet sentiment."

Brian laughed heartily. "Get used to it, sis. That's what women like, at least every woman except you."

"I'll never understand."

"Well, either date another butch or learn."

She sighed. "Okay, love guru, tell me what to do."

"It's simple. Find a romantic card with a nice message. Don't get one that goes on forever and whatever you do, don't get a funny card. At this stage in your relationship Ari would probably doubt your sincerity if a ridiculous cartoon character recited a trite limerick to her."

"What about a gift?"

"You'll need to go somewhere else. Stuffed bears and chocolates are for amateurs. You bought her a necklace for her birthday so a bracelet would be a good choice for Valentine's Day."

"Like in the shape of the heart?"

He chuckled, obviously pleased. "You're catching on, grasshopper. Gotta go claim my foot rub," he added before signing off.

She scanned the sparse rows of picked over cards. She spied one that met her brother's specifications. Just as she reached for it, an oblivious twiggy woman chatting on her cell phone plucked it from the stand and walked away.

She resisted the urge to shoot her and continued to search.

They all seemed redundant in words and tone, and she couldn't decide. She grabbed a linen card with gold script and suddenly felt as though she was being watched. She whirled around, and a flash of blue stepped into another aisle.

Someone's following me. The card still in her hand, she maneuvered into the next aisle but the blue jacket was gone. She paid for the card and headed back into the mall and a Macy's. All she wanted was a scotch—her motivation for quick decisiveness as she purchased a simple gold bracelet in record time.

"Done," she said to herself, climbing back into her truck. As she drove toward the mall exit she glanced in her rearview mirror just as a figure in a blue jacket and baseball cap darted into the parking lot.

Wertz pulled the Ford roadster up to the immense wrought iron gate that lined the Glick property. He pressed the intercom as Ari listened to the whir of the closed circuit television camera turn toward the car. The lens stared at them for several seconds before the gate slowly rolled open. The old car rumbled up the side of the hill, following a gravel path through the dense foliage around the property. The road ended in front of a four-car garage that sat underneath a house supported by strong metal stilts holding it in the air for a better view of the valley.

She'd debated canceling the appointment, firing her client and sharing her suspicions with Lorraine. She'd thought about involving Molly, but purchasing a flask meant he was guilty of nothing except perhaps private drinking. He didn't notice her uneasiness, his mind focused on acquiring the Glick house.

She gazed up at the structure, an intricate balance of steel and wood that seemed to blend naturally into the mountain. They stepped onto a long porch and she realized she was dangling over a ravine that separated the house from the main entryway. Glass windows afforded them a view into an amazing living area. She couldn't wait to see the inside of the house. They were greeted by Jacob Glick himself when they rang the bell.

"Good evening," he said. "Please come in."

He led them into the living room, and she heard the gentle sound of rain. She looked over her shoulder and saw the source— sparkling blue water poured in from beneath a glass wall and cascaded down several steps before emptying into a pond filled with exotic fish. The entire scene was serene. Glick motioned to the couch. Ari deliberately chose a chair where she could study the falling water.

"Now, please explain to me the purpose of your visit."

She looked at Wertz, expecting him to take the lead, but he raised his eyebrows at her. She was the real estate agent, and if she wanted a commission, she'd have to do the dirty work.

She smiled pleasantly at Glick. "We appreciate you taking the time to see us, especially on such short notice."

He nodded and returned the smile. "You're welcome."

"We're here because Mr. Wertz saw your home and instantly fell in love with it."

"I see. I hope you're not here to make a sales pitch since I have no interest in selling Serendipity. This place belonged to my brother, and it's the only memory of him that I have. While I could certainly make a fortune on its sale I just couldn't leave."

"Sentiment aside," Wertz interjected, "I don't understand why you'd keep a place that's driving you deep into debt."

Ari shot him a glance, and Glick turned bright red. Obviously Wertz knew something she didn't.

"My financial affairs are none of your concern," Glick said evenly.

Wertz smiled smugly. "Oh, but they will be soon. Let's get down to it. You don't own the building that houses your little company, do you, Mr. Glick?"

He shifted in his seat and frowned. "No, we've been trying to buy it. I'm sure we'll be successful—eventually."

"Ah, but you see I already was."

Wertz removed a folder from his briefcase and held out a copy of what Ari assumed was a contract. "This contract indicates that I am now your landlord." He shook his head woefully while Glick read the document. "I just don't think I can let you stay when your lease expires in two months. I'm sure we could work something out and under certain circumstances, I'd be happy to sell the property to you at quite a bargain."

Glick studied the contract, his anger visible. When he glared at Wertz it was with a fury that made Ari shiver.

"How in the hell did you do this? I've been wrangling with the owners for over a year!"

Wertz shrugged slightly. "I'm a good businessman, and I made them an offer that was too good to pass up. I guess you didn't do that."

Glick crumpled the contract and stared at the floor. "I'm sure you know it would be impossible for me to find a place to house my business, not to mention the difficulty of moving all of the equipment."

"Hmm. Those would be two of the hurdles you'd obviously face," Wertz agreed. "There are definitely pitfalls to owning a dry cleaners. All those nasty federal regulations, too. This is quite the dilemma."

"You're a diabolical bastard, forcing me to choose between my home and my business!" Glick shouted.

Wertz feigned shock. "I'm doing no such thing. I'm merely offering you a way around your financial woes. I'd think you'd be grateful."

Glick jumped to his feet and yelled, "Get the hell out of my house! Right now!"

Ari was moving before he'd punctuated his sentence, but Wertz strolled behind casually glancing at the walls, imagining where he'd hang his artwork.

"Would you like to tell me what just happened?" she asked once he'd joined her in the car.

He twisted his head in her direction, his publicity face perfectly restored. "Ari, darling, life is full of choices. We'll give Mr. Glick some time to really think about my generous offer. And now I believe you owe me a dinner. I know I said you could pick, but I do know a wonderful place. Why don't you let me show you?"

She felt sick to her stomach. "Not tonight, Stan. Please take me back to my car."

They meandered down the driveway toward the lights of

the city. She craned her head around to get one final look at Serendipity. Jacob Glick stood in front of an enormous picture window with his arms folded, watching them descend the mountain.

They said nothing on their way back into Phoenix, but Wertz whistled most of the way. It was clear to her that he was capable of blackmail—but could he kill a man to get what he wanted?

His cell phone rang, and he greeted Candy. His expression shifted and he frowned. When he hung up, he didn't whistle again. He was clearly upset, and she was relieved he didn't want to talk.

Yet as he returned to the Day Arbor neighborhood and pulled up to her SUV, the nearby streetlight illuminated his pleasant expression. *Maybe he's bipolar.*

"Please come by my house around ten tomorrow. I believe we can finish our business then. I'm certain Mr. Glick will be ready to sell. And although I've done most of the dirty work, I'm still willing to pay you a commission."

She knew he expected her to be grateful and say thank you, but as she turned away he roared into the driveway. She didn't care and couldn't wait to be rid of him.

CHAPTER TWENTY-THREE

The phone awoke Molly from her drunken stupor. She glanced at the clock. It was Andre or Ari. No one else would call this early.

"Nelson."

"We got a lead on Selena Diaz. They're out in Gila Bend staying with a friend."

"How do you know?" she said, reaching for the aspirin.

"Came in through the front desk early this morning. I just got here when Brewster waved me over. Somebody dropped the tip on his desk while he was in the can. It gave an address and mentioned the name Diaz, written in a woman's handwriting. That's all anybody knows."

"That's really fishy, Andre. It could be a wild goose chase."

"I don't think so. Whoever left that note wanted to make sure

Brewster found it. I'd say it's somebody with inside information, and we should check it out."

She closed her eyes, certain that he was right and wishing she'd skipped her evening at Hideaway.

"Okay, I'll be there in twenty."

They spent the fifty-mile drive to Gila Bend discussing the 6815 address and the mole. Andre had cruised past both of the possible addresses the day before but noticed nothing suspicious.

"They all looked alike," he said. "They're those typical suburban stuccos with red-tile roofs."

"Just like my parents' place," Molly added, thinking of the cookie-cutter community she visited twice a month for dinner.

"I didn't see anything unusual, and the neighborhoods are decent. Lots of Toyotas and trucks in the driveways."

Molly sighed, wondering if it was a dead end. Andre must have sensed her frustration as he reached over and squeezed her shoulder.

They said little else as they motored down the highway passing the Lewis Prison. Gila Bend was the halfway point between Phoenix and Yuma and often a stopping point for tourists and travelers on their way to San Diego.

Andre slowed to thirty-five as the highway suddenly became the main drag of the town. Just past the McDonald's they turned into a residential area and searched for the house. The neighborhood reminded her of South Phoenix. She realized how easy it would be for the Diaz family to blend in with the migrant workers that populated the town.

"I'm wondering if Hector Cervantes didn't do a little detective work for us," Andre said absently.

Finding the house proved difficult since none of them had visible numbers. "How the hell does the mailman deal with this?" she muttered.

"He's probably been on the job for thirty years," he replied.

They pulled up in front of a run-down ranch house on a corner lot. Three cars were parked in the driveway, including a pickup like the one owned by Jose Diaz. A man emerged from the side of the house wearing a dark hoodie. Andre quickly pulled up behind the truck, startling the man.

"Jose Diaz?" Andre shouted.

"Who wants to know?"

She noticed the man's right hand went to his jacket, and she was sure his fingers were wrapped around the butt of a gun.

Andre held his revolver at the man's chest. "Police. I suggest you slowly put your hands in the air."

Jose Diaz did as he was told. Andre searched him and withdrew a Beretta from his jeans.

"What do you want?" Diaz asked. "I didn't do anything. That gun is just for protection. It's registered."

Andre stepped away with the gun. "Give it a rest, Jose. We just need to talk to Selena."

Panic turned to confusion. "Selena? Why?"

Molly stepped forward and joined her partner. "Mr. Diaz, my name is Detective Nelson and this is Detective Williams. Your daughter may have witnessed something that's important to our investigation. We need to interview her now. She's not in any trouble."

Diaz glanced at the house and shuffled his feet. "How did you find us?"

"We got an anonymous tip," Andre said. "And that means somebody knows where you are."

Diaz shook his head. "I didn't tell nobody. We just left and came out here. Friend of mine has this empty rental."

"Look," Molly offered, "You let Selena help us, and we'll tell the Gila Bend PD to keep an eye on you, okay?"

Diaz nodded in relief. "She's inside. We've been trying to make it look like no one's here."

He led them through the back door into the kitchen. A woman sat at the table breast feeding an infant and studying a large textbook that lay open in front of her. She looked up, surprised.

"This is my wife, Bonita." Molly and Andre nodded at the

scared woman. "It's okay, honey," Diaz said. "They're police officers and they need to talk to Selena."

"This is about Maria, isn't it?"

"Yes," Molly said. "She may have some information that will help us catch Maria's killer."

Bonita Diaz's expression remained serious as she weighed the ramifications of involving her daughter in police business. "She's in the back bedroom watching TV," she told her husband.

Diaz disappeared down the hallway, calling for Selena. There was awkward silence as Bonita Diaz covered herself and burped the baby.

Molly's eyes drifted to the open book and the small print and charts that covered the pages. "Studying?"

Bonita's expression softened, and she nodded. "I'm about to take my nursing tests next week."

"Wow, I'll bet that's hard," Molly offered.

Bonita sighed and rocked her baby. "It is. I already told Jose that he's got to get past this nonsense with Big Paddy. I'm going back for my exams with or without him."

Molly smiled at the woman's determination. Bonita didn't have any problems standing up to the thugs her husband knew, and no one was going to keep her from her dream. Feet shuffled and Selena Diaz stood in the kitchen doorway, her father's protective arm wrapped around her shoulder. She wore a pink nightgown that fell to the floor and billowed around her slight frame.

Sensing her daughter's hesitancy, Bonita Diaz smiled with confidence, hiding her own concerns about the family's troubles. "It's okay, baby. These detectives are trying to find out who killed Maria, and they need your help. They think you know something."

Selena's eyes widened, and she shook her head. Molly crouched down and looked sympathetically into her eyes. "Selena, I know how much you cared about Maria. It's really hard to lose your best friend. I know because I lost mine." Molly paused and Selena stared at her. "It's true. My best friend was a policeman and a bad man killed him."

"Did he die?"

"Yes. He was shot during an arrest."

"Maria was shot," Selena whispered. "I told her I thought she was in danger, but she said I was stupid."

"Why did you think she was in danger?"

"Because of what she told me."

"What did she say?"

Selena glanced at her parents, who looked surprised. "Something happened when we went to the science center, but I promised not to tell."

Selena looked at Molly with hopeful eyes. Molly gently smiled. "Selena, I understand secrets between friends, but Maria's dead now and you may be the only person who can help us catch her killer."

"She told me about a bad man."

"Can you tell me what happened?"

Selena swallowed hard and bolted toward her mother. She fell into Bonita's arms and buried her face in her chest. Still cradling the baby, she gently smoothed her hair and whispered softly in her ear. Selena nodded and turned to face Molly.

"What did Maria say about the bad man?"

"We were at the science fair and she went back to the bus. When she came back to the group she was really scared. She said a man had chased her."

"Why?"

"Because she saw him hurt somebody."

"Did she tell you about that?"

"Uh-huh. She'd gone back to the bus in the parking garage. She heard yelling and looked out the window. There was a guy pushing another guy against a wall and he told him if he didn't listen, he would be sorry."

"Maria saw this?"

Selena nodded. "She said the one guy was really scared and he was begging the mean guy not to hurt him. Then the bad man stepped away like he was trying to be his friend."

"And then what happened," Molly coaxed.

Selena paused and cocked her head to the side. "Maria said it was weird. They got into the car for a little while and then the car horn went off and the bad man got out and looked around. That's when he saw Maria watching him."

"So what did he do?" Molly asked, already knowing the answer.

"He got really angry and started to run at her. So Maria ran out of the bus and back to the front of the science center where we were eating lunch. She was out of breath and talking really fast. That was when she told me."

"Why was she on the bus?"

She fidgeted in her seat. "I'm not supposed to tell."

Molly leaned close, and put her hand on the kitchen table. "Selena, you can tell me. I won't say anything. I can keep a secret."

She looked at her mother, who nodded at her daughter. "Raul asked her to go back to the bus with him. They sneaked away from the group."

"Why did Raul want Maria to go back to the bus with him?"

Her cheeks reddened and she smiled slightly. "He wanted to kiss her."

Molly took a deep breath. "I see. So they liked each other."

"Well, I think Raul liked her more than she liked him. He was her boyfriend, but nobody knew that except me. She let him kiss her once but then when he wanted to keep doing it, she told him no and he got mad and ran off the bus."

"So after Maria told you about the man did she tell an adult?"

Selena shook her head. "Uh-uh. She just pointed at the guy."

Molly's heart lurched. "You actually saw the bad man?"

"Yeah. He ran out of the garage and he looked around like he was trying to find Maria."

"And did he see Maria?"

"Yeah. When he looked over at her, he stared at her and she just folded her arms. She wasn't afraid of him."

"What did he do next?"

"He just walked away. The teacher was lining us up."

"Would you recognize him if you saw him again?"

Selena nodded. "I know who he is."

Molly and Andre exchanged glances. "Who, Selena?" Andre asked.

"That man on TV. The Hometown Grocery guy."

CHAPTER TWENTY-FOUR

Ari meandered through traffic thinking about what she would say to Stan Wertz. He'd called at eight to confirm their ten o'clock appointment, gloating about his victory over Jacob Glick. As he'd predicted, Glick was willing to sell Serendipity for an outrageous price. She'd spent the entire conversation fuming over his tactics but realized there was nothing she could do. She rationalized that she'd earned her commission simply by tolerating his advances and enduring his sliminess. She'd write the contract, take it to Glick for his signature and file it. Then she would be done with Stan Wertz.

She'd almost cancelled on him, but there was no hard evidence to suggest he'd done anything sinister. She'd share her suspicions with Molly that night, although the thought of ruining Valentine's Day didn't appeal to her. He was probably guilty of nothing more than ruthless behavior, and while that was certainly unethical, it wasn't illegal.

Her cell phone rang. *Biz*. She took a deep breath and answered with a casual, "Hello?"

"Happy Valentine's Day, gorgeous."

She felt her cheeks flush. "Is there something I can do for you, Biz?"

Biz sighed. "All business. I get it. Now that I've signed on the dotted line you won't have anything to do with me."

She sounded pathetic, and Ari pushed away the guilt that instantly surfaced. "Biz, we don't have a personal relationship, remember?"

"What about that kiss?"

"That was business, too!" she said, much louder than she intended. Biz was clearly under her skin, and what she needed was distance—particularly on Valentine's Day. "Look, I'll call you next week. Right now I'm on my way over to Stan Wertz's for the last time. He's found a house, and we're writing a contract. I'm almost done with him."

There was a pause—she was sure Biz was thinking.

"Are you sure this isn't dangerous, Ari? Given our suspicions about him and Edgington?"

She shook her head. "There's nothing to be suspicious about. He knows nothing, and as you said yourself, it's probably all coincidental. Gotta go."

She hung up before Biz could respond and reached for the air conditioner. It was February and she was hot. *You're more afraid of Biz than Wertz.*

When she pulled up to the house, that same wonderful feeling came over her again. She loved this house. She couldn't believe it had only been five days since she'd walked up the path with Lorraine. She was shocked when she rang the bell and Stan himself opened the door to let her in.

"Ari," he said warmly. "Please come in."

He gestured toward the living room and shut the door behind her. She noticed the stillness that surrounded them. "Where's Dora?"

"Today's her day off, and I must make do myself," he said dramatically, leading her into the living room.

His joke sounded forced. She immediately sensed that something was off. Once they were seated he fidgeted in his chair. He didn't ask his questions in rapid-fire delivery as he usually did, as if time was a valuable commodity that he couldn't waste. Instead he seemed relaxed, almost chatty. He made small talk about the weather, asked her about business and engaged in pleasantries she thought he found tiresome. Suddenly his face turned stony.

"Ari, Candy tells me that you came back to the office after our little meeting the other day. You and your friend?"

The shift was unexpected, and she was momentarily caught off guard. "I did. I'd left a folder in your office." She gazed straight into his eyes and didn't let her voice waver.

He offered a sad smile. "I didn't find a folder, Ari. I always check my office thoroughly before I leave." His voice was disappointed, like a parent who just learned his kid was smoking pot.

"I assure you, it was there."

He gave her a dark look. "I don't believe you. I'd like you to be honest with me. I would expect nothing less of my real estate agent, the person I'm trusting with an incredibly important decision. You would agree, wouldn't you? I should trust you implicitly?"

"Absolutely. And I would never lie to you about your transaction."

"What about anything else?" he asked acidly. "Ari, my dear, I fear you've found yourself in the middle of something you can't understand, and you've uncovered something that must remain secret. In essence, you're a liability."

She bolted from the chair and ran for the door. When she twisted the knob, she realized he had engaged a two-way deadbolt. She heard him jingling the keys as he approached, cornering her in the small entryway. She assessed her options while he stood there grinning with a small caliber revolver in his hand. There was no way out.

"Now why don't we step back into the living room?" His voice was civil, almost kind. "It's so rude to have conversations in the entryway." He casually looped his arm through hers and led her to a wooden chair near the window. You'll have to excuse me for tying you up. I'm rather certain our bond of trust is irrevocably broken."

He reached behind the chair and withdrew a length of cord and duct tape from a nearby basket. He was clearly prepared and had plans for her. Her purse was over on the sofa and contained her pocketknife, but she didn't know how she could get to it. She needed more time to make a plan.

"So what do you think I know, Stan?"

"I think you suspect that I killed Warren Edgington and Maria Perez." Her surprise wasn't lost on him. "Oh, so perhaps you didn't know that I hired someone to kill that little girl. Even I have my limits, but I know you've been searching for evidence to implicate me in Warren's death. Candy may be a little tramp," he added, "but she knows when she's being played. While your hussy friend seduced her, you searched my office. You left a few things out of place and I imagine you came across something important."

He watched her closely and saw the truth before she could hide it.

He shook a finger at her. "That's what I thought. You've been a bad girl, Ari. You see, I pay Candy quite well and satisfy her every kinky need. She's more faithful than a dog."

As he secured the final knots she found her hands and feet bound to the wooden spokes of the chair. The knots were complicated sailor's knots—as a wealthy businessman he'd probably spent time yachting.

"There we go. That should hold you." He moved to the couch and rummaged through her purse. "Now, let's see what we have in here." He quickly found her pocketknife, cell phone, nail file, and most importantly, the copy she'd made at his office. "Ah, this is what I need."

He folded the pages and tossed them between the fireplace logs. She closed her eyes momentarily as he lit a match and destroyed the only physical evidence that tied him to the murder of Warren Edgington.

He clapped his hands together and smiled. "That's done. There's only one loose end—that's you."

Hoping to buy some time, Ari said, "Why'd you kill him? He was your friend, wasn't he?"

"Because he got in the way," he growled, "or rather his newly-found conscience got in the way. Before he got Candy pregnant he was the perfect stooge. Laws, codes and ordinances meant nothing to him. We had the perfect setup going. Then his lust for Candy turned into *love*," he said mockingly.

Ari thought she was starting to see the whole picture. "So you brought Candy and Edgington together?"

He grinned. "It was brilliant. I wanted the land at that corner. I *needed* it, Ari. It's going to make millions! FoodCo will lose its foothold in the east valley when I open the Hometown City Center. But timing was everything." He sat down on the edge of the coffee table in front of her. "I had a very short window of opportunity, and I wanted to open at Christmas."

"That's impossible," she said, knowing that it would take months just to move the plans through all of the necessary regulatory channels.

"Ah, but I have some powerful friends in the city planner's office. Remember what I told you, Ari. Every man has his price."

"Apparently you misread Warren's," she said, almost regretting the words as they left her mouth.

"Apparently," he said. "After I introduced him to Candy he was willing to do whatever it took to sell me that land, cut whatever corners were necessary, including violating landlord and tenant laws with a little cash."

"So you bribed the tenants into an early exit?"

He snorted. "The furniture guy was happy to go, and so were a few others. Those moronic manicurists couldn't be convinced so their shop was going to have a little *accident*. That's when Warren lost it. He refused to be a part of it and threatened to go to the authorities. He wouldn't listen to reason."

She tugged at the knots, but they wouldn't give. "How did you kill him?"

He leaned forward. "I didn't kill him. Technically he killed himself. After our little argument, which you unfortunately witnessed, I followed him out to his car. I was angry, and I shoved him against the wall. We were shouting. I thought we were alone."

"But you weren't," she said, suddenly realizing why Maria Perez was killed. "That little girl saw you."

He looked away momentarily. "Yes, it was a shame." He sighed and continued his story. "I knew Warren wouldn't relent, but he was a sucker when it came to friends so I said I was sorry and he forgave me instantly. He'd already had a few drinks, alcoholic that he was, and I coaxed him into the car and offered him the flask. We talked for a few minutes while he drank an incredibly lethal concoction that I'd created. I told him Candy didn't love him and was getting an abortion at that very moment. He started to cry and drank more. Eventually he passed out, and his head hit the steering wheel. I left the note and got out quickly—and saw the little girl. I chased her, but she ran back to her group." He stared at her, his eyes slits. "The rest I guess you know."

"I can't believe you killed two people over *land*. You're the Hometown Grocery guy, for God's sake!"

He just shook his head and chuckled. "Ari, you haven't been listening to what I've tried to tell you all along. Competition is fierce and FoodCo has given me no choice. Their mission is to drive me out of business and take over the entire shopping industry. It's so cliché, but this business is my life. Every day is about marketing the products, creating PR to draw in new customers, riding the tough times, profit and loss margins and so much more. People are counting on me. I took a little second-hand market and turned it into a corporation. You have no idea what that entailed or what I sacrificed. To lose it would be to lose my existence. It would mean that I have wasted my entire life." He spoke slowly and paused for emphasis. "I'm not a murderer. FoodCo drove me to extreme measures."

"That is such a pathetic excuse," she whispered.

He glared at her. "That won't be your problem much longer. You'll worry about very little." He caressed her face and smiled. "I *am* very sorry that we never got to have our dinner. I'm certain that after a bottle of wine from my special collection, you'd have been willing to give heterosexuality a try."

She bit her tongue and said nothing. Angering him further wouldn't help her situation.

He went into the kitchen and when he returned, he carried a white rag in his hand.

"No!" she cried as the room went dark.

CHAPTER TWENTY-FIVE

While Andre secured a warrant for Stan Wertz, Molly reviewed the Perez file. As was her habit she began drawing circles, working from the center out—the center being the victim, who no longer was Maria Perez but Warren Edgington. Since childhood she'd had an uncanny knack for creating nearly perfect freehand circles of many sizes. Now she filled the paper with several of them, drawing connecting lines, which represented the various people involved and the possible relationships that might exist.

"I'm glad you have time to doodle, Nelson," Ruskin said sarcastically.

She looked up from her desk, so involved in her thoughts that she'd failed to notice him. She ignored his dig and held up the pad. "I've got a theory. Stan Wertz wants a Hometown Center.

He wants property in Chandler and gets Edgington to sell to him." She picked up a sheaf of papers. "These were filed with the Chandler City Planner's Office and from what I can tell they skipped a ton of steps."

"So what?" Ruskin barked. "What does that have to do with murder?"

She tried to remain calm. "I'm not sure what went wrong, but it all came to a head that day at the luncheon. That's where Ari saw them arguing and then Maria Perez saw Wertz leaving the car. She and her boyfriend had gone back to their school bus for a little kissing action. Wertz didn't realize that other people were around. According to Maria's best friend, she saw him threaten Edgington, then act friendly with him, inviting him into the car. But when Wertz got out Edgington didn't. I think we can assume that by then he was dying or dead, his head resting on the steering wheel and the car horn. So Wertz sees Maria Perez and chases her out of the parking garage, but she runs to her school friends. He knows she'll eventually tell so he's got to do something about it. Maybe he was too squeamish to kill a kid or maybe he didn't think he could get close to her again since she'd seen him, but for some reason he hires a hit man who takes her out, and none of it can be traced back to him—"

"Except through a hearsay witness whose testimony will never be allowed," Ruskin interrupted.

"That's true," she agreed.

He scratched his head and pointed at her. "Get the warrant and get out of here!" he barked.

He turned to go and nearly crashed into Biz Stone.

She swallowed hard as her anger swelled. "What are you doing here?"

Biz dropped into a chair across from her nervously tapping her foot.

"I'm sure you're swamped with Maria Perez, but I've got something you need to know about Warren Edgington. That was originally your case, wasn't it?"

At the mention of his name she sat up in her chair. "What do you know?"

"His wife thinks he was murdered so she hired me."

She quickly flipped to a new page of her tablet, hiding her notes from Biz's view. "Have you found out anything that would support that theory?"

"Possibly. You found a flask, right?"

"Yes," she answered guardedly. "Where are you going with this, Biz?"

"I think the murderer tricked Warren Edgington. Did you know he was an alcoholic?"

She shook her head. "Nobody described him that way."

Biz snorted. "That doesn't mean anything. Alcoholics do a great job of walking the line."

Her temper slowly burned. "So what do you think happened?"

"I think that the killer lured Edgington into the car, offered him a drink from a flask filled with booze and drugs and waited. It looks like suicide. It's really murder."

She looked at Biz, the thoughts coming at her from all directions, recognizing how neatly Biz's explanation fit with her hypothesis and it totally jived with what Maria Perez told Selena Diaz. She tapped her pencil on the pad deciding how much she should reveal to a civilian. Finally she set the pencil down and folded her hands in front of her.

"Do you have any evidence to prove your theory?"

Biz shifted uncomfortably. "I do but unfortunately it wasn't obtained using proper or legal procedure."

Her face darkened. "Damn it, Stone! If you've screwed up my case, I'll have you arrested!"

Andre burst into the room, waving the warrant. "I've got it, Mol. Let's go get Wertz."

Biz shot a glance at Molly. "Wertz? Stan Wertz? Is he the one who killed Edgington?"

"Very possibly. What do *you* know about him?" Molly asked caustically, leaning across her desk.

"I know that your girlfriend's at his house right now."

Molly threw the bubble light on the top of the Chevy

Caprice and weaved through the noontime traffic. She'd already dispatched several units to Wertz's house, but she'd instructed them to wait for her to arrive since it was most likely a hostage situation. She asked Biz a few questions, and it became clear that Ari and Biz had been investigating Warren Edgington's death—and Ari had said nothing to Molly. Her emotions blended into a sick knot in her stomach, her anger swirling side by side with her fear that Ari was already dead or gone from the house.

She glanced at Biz, her jaw set into a serious expression. She could only imagine how well she knew Ari—she immediately chastised herself for letting her relationship paranoia surface at such an inappropriate time. Still, Ari had kept secrets. She also wanted to know how Ari had acquired the incriminating evidence against him, evidence she had withheld from her. That was a crime.

They whipped through the streets of Day Arbor, Molly watching for the inevitable small children who might be playing on their bikes in this overpriced historic neighborhood. She didn't need to check the address to know which house belonged to Stan Wertz since three police cars had pulled up in front of the historic home and Ari's SUV hugged the curb. She and Biz jumped out and found the first officer on the scene.

"No one has come in or out," he reported. "What do you want us to do Detective?"

"I want to check the property first, then we'll move in."

She took three steps before an explosion shook the street and a ball of fire rose from the back of the house. Smoke filled the air, black and orange tongues licking the neighboring trees while flames engulfed the western side of the house.

"Ari!" Molly wailed.

She ran until two policemen grabbed her and forced her back to the sidewalk. Clouds of smoke masked the flames and the screaming sirens of the fire engines soon corrupted the quiet street. She focused on the west side of the house covered in thick, foggy air. Pieces of the roof dropped onto the grass and she saw smoldering Bermuda grass in the side yard.

She couldn't move. She couldn't focus. She should be directing the officers but for some reason she was sitting on the curb, watching the firemen break down the front door, EMTs rushing into the house and Biz talking to an officer. She looked up at the sky, a mottled gray that eclipsed the sun. She found the effect mesmerizing.

"Molly! Molly, get up!" Biz was shouting.

She tilted her head in Biz's direction, the private investigator's silhouette hovering above her. "Where's Ari?"

"C'mon. They found her. She's alive! Molly, she's alive!"

Biz pulled her upright and held her steady until her wobbly knees stopped shaking. "Look at me, Molly." Biz stood in front of her, cradling her face in her hands. "Molly!" she barked.

"Yeah," she replied. "I'm with you."

"Did you hear what I just said?"

"Yeah. Ari's okay," she croaked, the tears streaming down her face.

"That's right. Now get it together. You need to check on your girlfriend and start acting like a police detective. This is a crime scene, Nelson. People are watching you."

The lecture had the desired effect, and the haze lifted like the smoke rising above the trees. She quickly assessed the situation realizing the fire was mostly out and had not jumped the hedge.

"Over there," Biz directed, pointing to the side of the house.

Ari was being led out by two burly firemen, an oxygen mask covering her face. It seemed as though she was floating and Molly realized the firemen were practically carrying her.

They took her to the back of an ambulance where several paramedics checked her vital signs. Molly's knees went weak at the sight of Ari wrapped in a fire blanket, shaking and frightened. When she looked up and saw Molly, she started to cry.

Molly nodded at Steve Jones, a paramedic she knew well. "Detective Nelson, do you know this woman?"

"She's my girlfriend."

"How is she?" Biz asked.

"She'll be fine," Jones reported. "The perp knocked her out with chloroform. We found her tied to a chair in the house, but she hadn't been harmed, at least not yet. I'm glad we got here when we did. Five more minutes and she might not have made it. Fortunately she's just suffering from smoke inhalation."

The paramedic taking Ari's blood pressure nodded at Jones, who motioned all of them to step back. Molly knelt in front of Ari and took her into her arms.

"My baby," Molly whispered.

"Honey, I'm sorry." Her voice was raspy from the smoke, and she coughed violently.

"Shush," Molly said. "Don't say anything. All I care about is you. We'll talk about everything else later."

They gazed at each other and Molly caressed her cheek. "I have to get to work. If you're strong enough, I need you to give your statement to Andre and I want Biz to drive you home. I'll see you tonight, okay?"

"Go," Ari managed.

She lowered the oxygen mask over her beautiful face and stepped back.

The paramedics swarmed around her again and she turned away to see Biz talking to one of the rookie officers. As she approached the rookie slunk away, well aware that he had been caught leaking information to a civilian.

"So what happened?" she asked sarcastically. She folded her arms and smirked.

Biz started to shrug her shoulders, but Molly cast a knowing look and Biz sighed. "Don't be mad at him, Nelson. He's just a kid. He's still learning not to fall for flattery or the charms of women."

She rolled her eyes and glanced back at Ari who was sipping water from a cup.

"Anyway," Biz continued, "I guess justice was served."

She turned back to Biz, a quizzical look on her face. "What do you mean?"

"Stan Wertz is dead."

It took four hours before the fire crew would allow her into the backyard. The charred remains entombed scattered pieces of Wertz's Ford Roadster. According to the fire marshal the car bomb detonated when he turned the key in the ignition, preparing to take Ari's limp body to wherever he intended to dump her. Molly pretended to listen, her mind still reeling from almost losing Ari.

She turned toward the damaged house. The entire west side was burned and she could see into the rooms, huge gaping holes in the wood affording her a view of the blackened interiors. She imagined the house could be restored eventually, but it was pathetic to see such a majestic structure in this state.

Andre rushed toward her and motioned to the street, where throngs of neighbors, bystanders and media stood behind the police lines. They walked to the front, avoiding the crime scene investigators as they searched for any clues to the identity of the bomber.

"Did you take Ari's statement? Is she okay?" she asked impatiently.

He nodded. "She's pretty weak, but her voice is coming back. She's just shook up. Wertz lured her over here. She had some evidence that could have incriminated him in the murder of Warren Edgington, and he found out about it."

Molly looked shocked. "Where did she get that?"

He paused, knowing his partner wouldn't like the answer. "She stole it from his office."

"Damn it!" She jammed her hands into her pockets, wanting very much to punch a wall or shake Ari senseless. She took a deep breath and returned her focus to the crime scene.

"I don't think they'll solve this one," he noted. "And I don't care since we just saved the taxpayers a ton of money."

"Me either," she agreed.

"But I think I know who planted that bomb." She stopped walking and stared at Andre, who pointed into the throng of ogling bystanders.

Molly strained to see individual faces against the western sun. A crowd of neighbors had gathered, craning their necks toward the smoldering house, pointing and whispering to each other. Her eyes found two Hispanic men at the back of the crowd— Hector Cervantes and Franco Perez. Neither seemed interested in the drama unfolding, but when Cervantes saw Andre point in his direction, he tapped Perez on the shoulder and whispered.

Both of them turned and stared at Molly before retreating down the street.

Andre glanced back at Molly with a slight smile. "What is it that Hector Cervantes does at his day job?"

"He's a mechanic."

CHAPTER TWENTY-SIX

Against the advice of the paramedics Ari refused to go to the hospital for observation. Biz gently lifted her into the SUV and took her home. She remembered nothing after Wertz covered her mouth with the chloroform. She'd awakened when the house was on fire, gasping for air. Then the firefighters burst into the room.

She closed her eyes and leaned back against Biz's warm body. They sat on the sofa, a bottle of tequila between them. Biz had first offered her a cup of tea but when she'd made a face, Biz found the liquor cabinet.

Ari grabbed the bottle by the neck and took a hefty swig. She was halfway to drunk and didn't care. *Maybe this is why Molly enjoys alcohol so much.*

The doorbell rang and Biz returned with Ari's father. He

stood in the center of the room, his hands on his hips, looking like a cop. Only his face wrinkled with worry betrayed the father in him.

"Are you all right?" he asked evenly.

She nodded. "Yeah, I'm fine. I was just in the wrong place at the wrong time."

He stared at the floor, and she knew he didn't know what to do. Lucia was always the comforter, the supporter. Jack kept his distance, detached from emotional situations.

"Is there anything I can get you?"

"No, Dad, I'm fine. Biz is taking care of me."

Jack studied her. "You're the girlfriend?"

Biz reached over to shake his hand. "No, sir, I'm just a friend. Biz Stone."

He seemed relieved. "Oh." He looked around and cocked his head to the side. "Where's your girlfriend?"

"She's working, Dad. She'll be here in a while."

"Um, okay. Well, I may stay in town for another couple days."

Ari shook her head. "You don't need to do that. I'm fine. There's no need for you to change your flight."

Jack shrugged and shifted his weight from one foot to the other. "It's not a big deal. I'm retired. Remember?"

They stared at each other, and she sensed that he could read her feelings. She didn't want him to stay, *couldn't* want him to stay. It would be submission, an invitation to a relationship she wasn't ready to have.

"Besides," he continued, "I was going to anyway. Sol invited me to the Suns game this weekend. He's got courtside seats."

Ari raised an eyebrow. "Against the Lakers? That must have set him back quite a bit."

"Exactly. How could I refuse?"

Ari cracked a smile. "Well, since we were supposed to have lunch today maybe we could do it tomorrow instead?"

Jack grinned. "That'd be great. I'll call you. I'm thinking barbeque."

Ari groaned, and Jack laughed as he strolled out the door.

Biz rejoined her on the couch and snuggled against her. "I like your dad."

"He's a character."

Biz stroked her hair and kissed the top of her head. Ari knew she should say something. She should push Biz away and insist that she go sit in the stuffed chair across the room. But she was too tired and Biz smelled too good. The tequila relaxed her, and she drifted off to sleep. She awoke to Biz shaking her.

"Hey, you looked like you were starting to have a nightmare. Are you okay?"

"I'm fine," she lied. "How long was I out?"

"About an hour."

Suddenly everything hit her at once—her kidnapping, nearly dying and dealing with her father. "It's been a hard day..." Her voice cracked and she sobbed.

Biz hugged her tightly. "I know."

She turned on her side and gazed into Biz's eyes. "I haven't thanked you. If you hadn't gone to talk to Molly, I'd probably be dead."

Biz caressed her cheek. "No thanks necessary. I enjoyed sleuthing with you, Ari Adams."

"Me too," Ari agreed.

Biz touched her forehead against Ari's. "I'm going to make a prediction."

Ari swallowed hard. Her mouth was dry, and she thought maybe the smoke inhalation from the afternoon was still getting to her. "What?"

"I'm going to kiss you again. And I predict it will be the softest kiss you've ever had."

Their lips touched and it was like falling into a warm ocean. She floated on the waves, as the kiss, which was the gentlest she'd experienced, rolled into another and another, carrying her with the tide. When Biz's tongue flicked against her own, she thought she might drown. She was helpless, unable to save herself.

"This is a hell of a way to end Valentine's Day."

Biz's lips pulled away, and she crashed into the shore. She looked up at Molly—her expression a mixture of revulsion and distress. She stood exactly where Jack had stood.

Ari suddenly realized that while her entire drunk psyche was focused on Biz's kisses and her metaphoric experience in the ocean, Biz had deftly unbuttoned her shirt and was caressing her breast.

She struggled to sit up. "Molly, please…" she begged, but Molly had already slammed the door before she could finish the sentence.

Continuous love songs blared from the Hideaway speakers as a few hundred drunken couples and singles celebrated the most romantic holiday on the calendar. Molly finished her fourth scotch and scanned the patrons, comforted that many of them wore looks of desperation or despair just as she did. *Misery definitely loves company.* It would have been smarter to slink back to her tiny apartment and drink there especially in light of her recent traffic stop, but she couldn't be alone. She owned a gun and the idea of sticking the barrel in her mouth had filled her head more than once in the past few hours.

"Dance with me," a voice commanded.

She swiveled her stool and faced Lola who wore a bright red dress with a plunging neckline. Her pushup bra displayed her large breasts inches from Molly's face.

"I don't dance," she said.

"Everybody dances."

She pulled her onto the dance floor and into a bear hug. Molly shuffled her feet and turned in a small circle while Lola pressed against her and long fingernails explored her hair.

She ignored the flirtations, her mind replaying the scene in Ari's apartment, over and over. She'd opened the door quietly, unsure if Ari was awake. She'd already decided they would celebrate Valentine's Day tomorrow if she was asleep, her hand absently slipped into her pants' pocket to feel for the bracelet.

The lights were on. She'd started to say something but was rendered speechless at the sight of Biz kissing Ari and fondling her breast. She'd stood there for several seconds, anger exploding in her heart. When she'd finally spoken, it was Biz who noticed her first. And Molly was absolutely certain a slight smile crossed her face—a smile of victory.

Lola cupped her face between her hands. "Hey, look at me."

Molly complied but said nothing. She had no desire to make friends.

Lola smiled in understanding. "I get it. You're hurt. Well, get over it. Half the women here tonight have been burned by someone. This party is as much a funeral for love as it is a celebration. For many of us love is dead." She traced Molly's lips with her index finger. "If I remember correctly, these lips can do amazing things."

Molly imagined Ari nestled in Biz's arms, her shirt unbuttoned, Biz's hand circling Ari's nipple, just as Lola circled her lips now.

"Let's go," Molly said, leading her through the back room, past numerous couples making out on the couches and in the corners. For a fleeting moment she thought of Jane and what she would tell Ari if she saw her with another woman—and she didn't care. Ari had made her choice. They went into the manager's office. As a regular and a cop Molly got special privileges.

"Where are we going?"

She ignored the question and opened an adjoining door into a large private bathroom. She pressed her against the wall and cupped her breasts. Lola cried out when Molly's lips found her nipples. She buried her head in her chest and started to cry. The pain was too much. Visions of Ari's smile filled her head. She dropped to her knees and pressed her face against Lola's stomach.

"Hey, baby, don't stop," Lola whined. She lifted Molly's chin and looked into her eyes. "You've been hurt bad. I can see that. You need to feel good again. I can help you."

The words made sense, and she gave a slight nod. Lola reached for her purse and withdrew a white pill from a pillbox. *Ecstasy or maybe speed.*

"Now, you take this, and I guarantee that you'll forget all about her, whoever she is. I'll make your troubles go away."

Like a child receiving Holy Communion, Molly opened her mouth and let the pill dissolve on her tongue. She fell against Lola and enjoyed the long fingernails stroking her hair. Within minutes her heart was racing, but she was feeling great. Nothing like scotch and drugs. She knew she was grinning and the woman smiled back.

"See? Better already. And since you're already down there, why don't you give me a little valentine?"

The music pulsated in her ears and she squeezed Lola's ass. They'd been dancing for an hour, and Molly had never felt so free. *Fuck Ari. Just fuck her.* When the music switched to a slow song, Lola pulled her to the bar for another drink. She'd lost track of how many she'd had—Vicky had said she was calling her a cab.

"Let's get out of here," Lola said and led Molly to her truck when Vicky wasn't watching. "Follow me to my place," she added with a deep kiss.

She jumped into a Mercedes convertible and headed for the exit. Molly's adrenaline was surging. She'd never felt this way. She *had* to have her. She ached for her. She hopped in the truck and blinked her eyes. A little voice reminded her about DUI, but when the voice turned into Ari's pleasant lilt, she sneered.

"Fuck her."

She pulled up behind the Mercedes just as it whipped into the center lane. She followed behind closely trying to remember the route to her place. Lola veered in and out of traffic and she struggled to keep up. Once she nearly crossed the center lane and an oncoming car sounded its horn and swerved away just in time.

"Shit!"

She knew she shouldn't be driving. She should forget the woman, pull into the nearest parking lot and sleep it off. *That's what you should do, Nelson. You know it.*

But she wanted to beat Ari. If Ari could cheat and throw

away their relationship, so could she. She hit the gas and zoomed behind the Mercedes, nearly rear-ending it. They'd driven east on Camelback Road around Camelback Mountain. Her body swayed with the twists and turns as she fought to stay in her lane. Suddenly Lola crossed two lanes of traffic and made a quick right onto Lafayette. Without looking or thinking, Molly followed— and overcompensated. She overshot the turn and panicked. She jerked the wheel and the truck spun until it plowed into a decorative wall that adorned the front of an expensive Spanish villa.

Her body shot forward into the deployed airbag. Before she passed out she remembered that in her hurry to rendezvous with Lola, she'd neglected to fasten her seatbelt.

Less than twenty-four hours after her truck crashed and she'd resigned from the police force, she sat at The Twenty Yard Line, a bar that cops and lesbians didn't frequent. She'd never again step through the doors of Oaxaca, the cop watering hole, and it would be a long time before she'd go to Hideaway either. It was all too humiliating.

The memories of Ari that had clouded her mind seemed distant and fuzzy compared to the larger than life visions of her stumbling out of the truck when the first on-the-scene police officers revived her. Despite forgetting her seatbelt she'd walked away without a scratch, the airbag preventing her from flying through the window and her inebriated state ensuring that she didn't tense up during impact. Lola was gone and she was alone.

They'd taken her weapon, handcuffed her and put her into a car. She was prepared for a trip to jail and was surprised when she was driven to police headquarters instead and led into Sol Gardener's office. He looked as though he'd been roused from sleep in his sweats and a baseball cap. The other cops left and closed the door behind them. She'd stared at his disappointed face and started to cry. He handed her a tissue and waited until she had her emotions under control.

"This is going to cost you, Nelson, but it could have been

much worse. After I got the call from Ruskin that you were in custody I woke up the mayor. He agrees with me that it wouldn't look good for the Department or the city if the detective that cracked the biggest homicide of the year went to jail. Also, that house you hit is in foreclosure. No harm, no foul. We're going to make this go away, Nelson. You're not going to jail but you're going to resign. Right now. Effective immediately.

She'd nodded and handed over her badge and gun, relieved that she wouldn't go down to booking, but already knowing her career as a police officer was over. She'd driven drunk and failed a breathalyzer by nearly two points.

Now, sitting on a stool at her neighborhood sports bar sipping a scotch, she wondered what she would do with her life. She still hadn't told her family. They would be crushed. Ari already knew and had left her a dozen messages, begging her to call, which she wouldn't. She glanced at the amber liquid inside the glass, swearing to herself that she'd never drink and drive again. The bar was only two blocks from her house so any night she got drunk she could just stumble home.

"I can't be arrested for that," she said to the glass.

For some inexplicable reason she'd brought the printouts of the unresolved number 6815 with her. She stared at the pages of numbers once more. There was a nagging feeling at the back of her brain—that somehow all of this was related—but her zeal for justice was depleted, and she just didn't care.

"Sorry, Itchy," she said, thinking of her informant who'd likely been killed by the mole.

The door opened and sunlight stretched across the dark room. Jack Adams strolled over and took the stool next to her. He ordered a beer and stared at the bar.

"How'd you find me?"

"Once I got your address I decided to check out the closest bars. This was my second stop."

She shook her head. "Why?"

He reached into his back pocket and withdrew his wallet. He flipped through his pictures and showed her an old studio portrait. It was faded and worn but the beautiful woman was remarkable and looked almost exactly like Ari.

"Isn't she absolutely incredible?" he asked, his voice full of admiration. "Isn't she the most gorgeous creature you've ever seen?"

She sipped her drink and refused to answer. Yes, Lucia was amazing, but no woman could ever compare to Ari. She closed her eyes, willing herself not to sob.

"Why won't you speak to her?"

She glanced up, surprised. "You knew? She told you we were involved?"

He shook his head, a sad expression on his face. "No, she didn't have to. I figured it out a few days ago. When I was in your office your cell rang and it played *Wipeout.* That was Ari's favorite song as a child. She used to stand around and dance to it." He chuckled. "What were the odds? Then she told me she was dating a cop so I just put it together."

Molly finished her scotch and put on her jacket. "That's some pretty good detective work. I think the department's hiring."

"What the hell happened, Nelson?"

That was a very good question, one she couldn't answer. Somehow everything had spun out of control. Now her career was over, and she'd lost Ari. She hopped off the barstool and threw some bills on top of the discarded printouts. She didn't care about moles and killers anymore.

Jack pointed to the printout. "What's this?"

"It's not important," she said, before staggering out of the bar.

CHAPTER TWENTY-SEVEN

He thought it was hot for February. Temperatures continued to hover in the high seventies when they belonged in the mid-sixties. He moved under the shade of the ramada and glanced at his watch. His connection was twenty minutes late. He'd just completed a call to Vince Carnotti, who was overjoyed at the dismissal of Molly Nelson. He'd escaped a close call, and his sigh broke the silence.

Losing Nelson was hard. She was a great cop—too good for collateral damage.

He heard the motorcycle before he saw it. The park was mostly empty as the visitors transitioned from families ending picnics to beer partiers who hadn't yet stopped by Circle K to get their alcohol. The motorcycle chugged to a stop next to his Infiniti and the rider dismounted—Biz Stone.

"Great meeting place, Sol. I think I swallowed a pound of dirt all the way up here."

Sol Gardener remained expressionless. He didn't care for Biz. He had nothing against lesbians but she was too butch, too hard. He much preferred Ari's classiness and Molly's androgyny. He saw her as crude and unrefined. Still, she'd come through and done her job.

He handed her an envelope of money, and she whistled when she glanced at the package of hundred dollar bills.

"Sweet. This'll pay for my new kitchen in the loft I just bought."

He turned to go, his business concluded. "I'll call you if I need anything else."

"Sol, wait a minute. You need a helper in the future, you find someone else. I'm done."

He crossed his arms and gave her a hard look. "Does this have anything to do with Ari?"

She shrugged. "I really care for her. That drunk Nelson didn't deserve her."

Sol exploded and pushed her against his Infiniti. "Listen, missy. Molly Nelson was a damn fine cop. Okay, she had a drinking problem, but she was a great person and our little scheme flushed her life down the toilet. So don't you ever say anything bad about Molly."

Biz put up her hands and moved away. "Sorry."

Sol took a step toward her, his finger pointed. "And don't you ever forget that Ari's my godchild. If you do anything to make her unhappy or jeopardize her life or career, I'll kill you. Know that."

CHAPTER TWENTY-EIGHT

The Hispanic man who hopped out of the taxi in front of 6815 West Windsong didn't notice the nondescript Buick down the street. He glanced over his shoulder before he jumped the fence into the backyard.

Jack pulled the binoculars away and reached for his clipboard. He recorded the activity on his log, one that was quite lengthy from the seven days he'd staked out the address. The comings and goings at the house suggested drugs, and he was impressed by the low-key operation. Only a tip from an informant, one like Molly's friend Itchy, would've led the police to the front door. Neighbors would never suspect.

He sighed deeply, still digesting the truth, which hurt him almost as much as Lucia's death. His best friend, his former boss, his mentor and Ari's godfather was on the take. And he was most likely responsible for the end of Molly Nelson's career.

She'd abandoned her spreadsheet on the bar as she staggered outside and he'd immediately noticed one of the entries—Duffek Turn. It was a kayaking term and Sol Gardener loved kayaking. It was Sol who convinced Jack to relocate there for his retirement, assuring him that when he retired he would join him and together they could start a kayaking company called Duffek Turn. It was too unbelievable to be a coincidence, but the obvious truth was numbing and forced him to action.

He staged his good-bye a week ago, allowing Ari to drop him off at the airport. No one knew he remained in Phoenix holed up in a Motel Six near the interstate. He'd spent much of his days and nights sitting in the rented Buick, watching, recording and waiting. So far he'd only seen low-level mules trafficking the goods.

He checked his watch. It was after sundown and time to move the Buick again. He made a U-turn and circled the block, deciding to park on the other side of the street in the opposite direction. He knew if he kept this up much longer he'd need a different rental car. There was no reason to take chances since he didn't know who actually *lived* in the house. He'd watched people come and go but couldn't spot the owner.

He circled the block and parked again just as an Infiniti pulled up into the driveway.

"Show me something," he murmured.

He grabbed his camera and positioned his enormous telephoto lens. When no one immediately emerged from the car he worried that he'd been made and was the victim of a setup. Just as he was about to put the rental in drive, a man flew out of the house and raced toward the car. The window opened and the man leaned inside. Jack's heart rate quickened as he held the shutter button down. He didn't think about what he was seeing. He only focused on recording the interaction between the underling bending over to receive his instructions from the powerful boss driving the Infiniti—Sol Gardener.

CHAPTER TWENTY-NINE

Ari and Jane rode silently through the neighborhood. Since her breakup with Molly, Jane had ceased her usual joking and sarcasm. A part of Ari was grateful for the silence—another part of her missed the normalcy.

And it would take a long time to get back to normal and forget Molly.

"Where are we going?" she asked impatiently.

"You'll see," Jane said with a slight smile.

She opened the paper and decided not to think about the mystery. On the front page of the local section was a wonderful human interest story, the reunion of Millicent and Laurel Jeffries.

"This is great," she commented with as much enthusiasm as she could muster. "How is Laurel adjusting?"

Jane nodded. "She's doing well considering that she hasn't seen her mother since she was a child. Millicent walked out on her when she was four, but I think they'll be okay."

Happy endings are nice. Jane turned into the Day Arbor neighborhood, and Ari's anxiety skyrocketed.

"Where are we going?"

"It's okay, honey. I need to show you something."

She wasn't surprised when Jane's Porsche stopped in front of Stan Wertz's ruined house. Lorraine's real estate sign had been removed although the familiar white post still stood in the ground at the edge of the cement walkway.

"Here we are!"

She sighed. "Why?"

"You'll see. C'mon."

Jane ignored her protests and bounded out of the Porsche. She fumbled through her purse until she pulled a key from its depths and opened the front door. Clearly Lorraine and Jane had planned something. Ari remained in the car, unwilling to play along. Jane waved with her natural enthusiasm, coaxing Ari to join her, but she just shook her head.

Jane entered the house and stuck her head out, grinning. Ari slightly smiled at her antics. She was certainly determined. A rumbling from behind the Porsche caused her to glance into the rearview mirror, just in time to see the enormous chrome grill of a Ford truck nearly kiss the Porsche's tail. Her heart skipped a beat momentarily as she thought of Molly, but when she turned around, Jane's good friend and handy dyke, Teri, hopped out of the cab with her tool belt slung around her hips.

"Hey, Ari. Are you getting out?" She offered her hand which Ari felt obligated to accept.

"I'm sorry about everything that happened," she said with a frown.

"Thanks."

The two of them studied the wounded structure. "This place is magnificent," Teri concluded. "I can only imagine what it looked like before the fire."

"It was wonderful," she said wistfully.

"Let's go in and find Jane," Teri suggested. "By now I

imagine she's searched through every closet and room in the place."

She chuckled and allowed Teri to guide her toward the front door.

"Jane!" Teri called.

"I'm up here!" Jane answered from the loft.

Teri vanished up the stairs leaving Ari to explore. Every stick of furniture had been removed, and the walls were dusted with the residue of ash and smoke. She looked at the beautiful Travertine tile, noticing that the women's footprints had left a trail up the stairs. The guest bedroom, guest bathroom and family room had been destroyed. She peered out at the backyard and glanced at the foundation of the car house, the only remnant of the place where she'd met Stan Wertz on the first day of their house hunting.

She wandered through the kitchen and through the doorway that led to the solarium. She was pleased to see it was unharmed and entirely unaffected by the explosion. She glanced at the detailed white woodwork that framed each of the large picture windows and the elaborate wainscoting extending to the floor.

"Ari, get up here!" Jane called.

She sighed and joined them upstairs. Teri was admiring the rounded archway that led from the master bedroom into the master bath. It was inviting, open and airy with French doors that led out to the Romeo and Juliet balcony. She imagined how wonderful it would be to lounge outside on Sunday mornings with coffee as she did now at her condo. She shook her head to erase the foolish notions.

"Jane, why are we here?" she asked impatiently.

She turned to her, a broad grin covering her face. "Do you like this place?"

Ari gasped and marveled at the magnificent bedroom. "It's unbelievable. Whoever built it was so meticulous, so caring."

"They were," Teri agreed. "The place was built in nineteen-ten by the Reynolds family. The father was one of Phoenix's original bankers. He wanted a place that wasn't far from downtown and had lots of trees."

"How do you know about the original owners?" Ari asked.

"I did some work for an elderly lady down the street. I went back there yesterday, and she told me all about the history of this house. I guess a lot of people have been inquiring about it."

She nodded in agreement. "Lorraine's phone has rung off the hook. People still think they can buy it. She's told the same story over and over, how it's part of the estate. Oddly enough I think it reverts to the wife."

"It does," Jane concurred. "And she wants to get rid of it—fast." Jane took her hand and led her into the loft that overlooked the spacious living room and the backyard. "In fact she's willing to sell it for only a fraction of what it's worth because three-fourths of the profits go to Wertz's family, and she could care less about any of them. Apparently they treated her as badly as he did. So she'd be happy to sell the place for five bucks if she could get away with it."

"How much does she want?" Ari asked, suddenly very curious. She had heard of such finds before, houses that were the victims of vicious divorces or contested estates. Vengeance became more important than wealth, and the lucky buyer was always a winner.

Jane produced a fax from her purse and flashed it under her nose. It was addressed to Lorraine and she scanned the five lines in which Beatrice Florence Wertz stated her ridiculously low asking price.

"She's kidding!" was all Ari could say.

"I thought so, too. And when Lorraine got this she thought about buying the place herself, but I convinced her that it should belong to you." Ari flicked her head from the fax to meet Jane's stare. "You need this, Ari. And the house needs lots of work but Teri will help you for a reasonable rate, and I know you've got a small fortune saved. Don't you think this place would be great for you?"

Her hands started to shake and the thought of finally owning a home, a dream she had helped so many others fulfill, suddenly made her sick to her stomach. "I don't know, Jane. I'm not sure I'm ready. I'm not sure I could live here after what happened."

Jane snorted and grabbed her friend's hand. She yanked Ari down the stairs and led her back to the solarium. She put her hands on her hips. "Say no to me here. I dare you to say no standing in this room."

Ari opened her mouth, but no words came out. She looked around unable to believe that she could buy the house. Jane was right. It was affordable, and she could entirely renovate it so that every memory of Stan Wertz was erased.

Teri leaned against the doorway, her muscular arms folded across her chest. Ari said, "Do you really think you can fix all of this?"

"I won't lie to you. It's going to take time and definitely some serious money because the insurance won't do it all. I'll need to hire some subcontractors. But when it's done it will be more incredible than it was before—"

"And worth about three times what you'll pay," Jane interjected.

"Absolutely," Teri agreed. "But I doubt you'll ever want to sell it once we get her back into her state of glory."

Ari smiled. That part was true. If she loved where she lived she could never imagine moving. She looked around the glass room trying to picture the house the way it was on the day she'd walked through the front door with Lorraine. She couldn't believe it was only a week before. The restoration would probably drain most of her savings, but it would be a fresh start and it would rejuvenate her. Perhaps that was Jane's plan all along.

"Okay," she said quietly.

Jane clapped her hands in glee and threw her arms around Ari. "That's wonderful! You're going to love it."

Jane raced out of the room already punching numbers into her cell phone. Ari chuckled as Jane told Lorraine about her news. Her best friend was more excited than she was. Teri led Ari into the west wing behind the vinyl tarps that separated the two sections of the house. She explained that Ari wouldn't want to live here until some of the major remodeling was complete. Once it was inhabitable she could move in while Teri completed the job. She tried to process everything Teri was saying about the timeline and the permits necessary, but her mind was numb from the idea of home ownership. They walked outside and examined the exterior. Teri was convinced that the structural damage was not serious. She gave Ari her card and departed with a wave to Jane as her old truck rumbled out of the neighborhood.

Ari took a final long look at the house that would be her first real home. It was inviting and warm. She knew each night when she pulled into the driveway she would feel content. She returned to the passenger's seat of the Porsche and reached instinctively for her cell phone to call Molly. She froze when she realized what she was doing.

It rang suddenly and she dropped it in her lap. *Biz*. She cleared her throat and took a deep breath. "Hello?"

"It's a pretty great house, don't you think?"

"What? How do you know about this?"

"I'm a private detective, remember? And I think you look hot in that red blouse you're wearing."

Ari's eyes widened as she glanced across the street. Biz's motorcycle sat against a curb a block away. She'd called every day since the blowup with Molly, but she'd changed. She wasn't flirtatious, and her comments were full of compassion and concern. It was a different side of Biz that she found incredibly appealing.

"Are you following me?"

"I just want to make sure you're okay," she admitted.

"I'm fine."

"Good. Do you like the house?"

A smile burst onto her face. "It's amazing. It's got this solarium that is unbelievable, and I love the loft. And…" She paused and took a breath. "You probably don't want to hear all of this."

"No, I do."

Suddenly the phone disconnected, and she heard the roar of the engine as the motorcycle sidled up next to her. She rolled down the windows, and Biz leaned through the driver's side.

"Come riding with me."

"I can't. I have things to do."

"Nothing that can't wait. Come on. I've got a spare helmet."

"No," she said simply.

Biz offered a sad smile. "I understand. But I'm not going to leave you alone, Ari Adams. I won't give up."

She roared away, and Ari gazed at her *home*, smiling at the prospect of new beginnings.

CHAPTER THIRTY

The south parking garage at Scottsdale Fashion Square was practically empty when Jack headed back to his rental. Only a handful of cars remained on a late Sunday night, and he guessed they belonged to mall security personnel out on their rounds. He watched the taillights of an Audi cruise through the exit, probably one of the few movie-goers who'd been in the theater with him watching the latest Anne Hathaway movie.

He'd needed a mental break from the drama that was swallowing his life, the one he was supposedly retired from. A movie always lifted his spirits, especially one starring a cute brunette. And Sunday nights were the best times to visit the theater—no crying babies with couples who couldn't afford a sitter on date night and no crowds either. He could extend his long legs into the aisle without tripping other patrons. He'd always pleaded with Ari and Lucia to go to the movies on Sunday nights because it was just so much more enjoyable. They'd pack up Ritchie, who usually slept through the whole thing, and go to the nine-thirty show. Those were some of his best memories.

The click of his boot heels resonated throughout the garage. The Buick was parked in a back corner. Always a cautious man, he deactivated the alarm and watched the overhead light come on. From what he could see there was no one else in the vehicle. He glanced over his shoulder before he got into the car.

He drove five feet and felt the car lurch. Something was wrong. He killed the engine and hopped out, walking the perimeter. He found the cause of his problem, a buck knife lodged between the treads of his back left tire. He shook his head. When he stood up, Sol Gardener faced him, a .38 special in his hand, a gun that Jack imagined probably belonged in the evidence room downtown.

"We're not gonna play any games here, are we Jack?" Sol asked. "Why don't you reach slowly into your jacket and give me your weapon."

He frowned and shook his head. His disappointment and hurt were evident. He couldn't meet Sol's gaze as he kicked his revolver toward him.

"How'd you find out?" Sol asked, picking up Jack's gun and sticking it into the back of his pants.

"Is it really important?"

"I suppose not, and I don't think you'd tell me anyway. For the record this is eating me up, the fact that you know. The fact that your opinion of me has changed—"

"Significantly," Jack whispered.

"Yeah, well, not all of us could be Big Jack Adams," he growled. "Not all of us were as smart or good looking or smooth."

He looked up and realized Sol had tears in his eyes, his gun hand unsteady.

"What are you talking about, Sol? You were with me every step of the way in the academy. We kept each other going. It was a competition, but you were my equal."

Sol snorted. "That was a million years ago. Judging from this moment, I'd say we're at very different places."

Although he could probably guess, he had to ask the question.

He had to hear the explanation from Sol. He folded his arms and leaned against the car. "I've got as long as you do, Sol. What the hell happened?"

"What *didn't* happen? Don't you remember the string of bad luck I had the first few years after the academy? I got stuck with that worthless partner and then Nancy got pregnant with Sol, Jr. She always said it was an accident, but I wasn't so sure. She wanted kids a lot sooner than I did. Then there were the complications in her pregnancy, and her mom got sick."

Snippets of memories tugged at Jack's mind, pieces of conversations over morning coffee or after roll call that he'd only paid courteous attention to. He'd never probed, never asked— and he'd certainly never suspected. But he could understand why a rookie might need extra cash.

"So it started all those years ago?"

Sol shrugged. Jack could see beads of sweat covering the top of his head.

"At first it was nickel and dime. Just a little shakedown. The big time stuff didn't come until later."

"You mean with Vince Carnotti."

"Yeah, he didn't know me in the beginning. I paid my dues. Eventually I got more responsibilities."

The air of pride in his voice disgusted Jack. He knew what *more responsibilities* meant to the mob, and he knew how well it paid. He read about corruption every day, but it seemed to happen in distant places, cities like Detroit or Chicago. The fact that Sol worked shoulder to shoulder with a mobster shocked him.

"How?" he thought to ask. "How could you get away with it for all of these years? You became the chief, for chrissakes! You closed more cases than anyone else."

Sol shrugged. "And did you ever think that was a little suspicious? Did you ever wonder how I juggled two or three big investigations at the same time? I had a little help. Sometimes evidence would just appear or a witness conveniently disappeared. How do you think I *got* to be chief? Did you ever wonder why it was me and not *you?*"

An odd sound pushed through his chest, and he realized before he could stop it that he was laughing. When he could finally control himself, he said, "I'm sorry. That isn't funny, but if you think I'm going to feel sorry for you, you're crazy. You're a disservice to every man or woman who's worn the badge. I'm ashamed to have called you chief. You think you're the only one who was ever tempted? Try having your little boy murdered in a convenience store, a wife sick with cancer and a daughter you nearly drive to suicide. I'd never trade my family for yours, Sol, but I'd have gladly traded problems—and I would've told the mob to shove it."

Sol's jaw set and his features darkened. His grip on the gun seemed to tighten, his hand grew steady. "Like I said, we can't all be the great Big Jack Adams."

"You never had to be me."

"Shut up Jack—"

"Or what? You'll shoot me? Isn't that the plan, Sol? Isn't that why you're here? When did you make me?"

Sol chuckled. "Second day. My guy at the house spooks easily. He's always moving through the rooms, peeking through the curtains. He calls me and tells me he's seen the same Buick parked in different spots. I came by so you could take my picture, and we could move this whole thing along."

Jack nodded. "So I guess we won't be retiring together in Oregon."

"No," Sol replied and Jack heard sadness in his voice. "Duffek Turn was never meant to be. I've got a place in the Caymans."

Jack looked around the garage, remote and still. "So how is this going down? Robbery gone bad? Carjacking?"

Sol nodded slowly. "First guess. The knife that's embedded in your tire is covered in the fingerprints of a known felon, one with a history of drug, robbery and assault charges. This crime against you will inevitably send him to prison for the rest of his life."

"Ah, a two-for-one. You save your hide and perform a civic duty in the process by removing one more scourge on society." He paused before adding, "I don't think anything can make up for what you did to Molly Nelson."

Sol frowned, and Jack knew he'd hit a nerve. "Nelson was a good cop. She should've left that informant's death alone. He was a total loser."

"And have you thought about how heartbroken Ari's going to be? She's lost her girlfriend and now her father?"

He sighed and scratched his head. "No chance you'd just let all this go and come with me? I don't think—"

A sudden crack pierced the silence, and Sol's gun clattered onto the concrete. A fountain of blood spewed from his arm. He stared in horror at the arch of red while Jack immediately kicked the gun away. Shock turned to pain, and he cried out. "You damn son of a bitch!"

Molly's voice boomed throughout the cavernous garage as she emerged from her hiding spot behind a green Honda thirty feet away. At the sight of her, Sol started to back away, holding his injured hand. She waved the pistol, but the hatred in her eyes was deadly.

"Did you forget I was the best shot on the range? Maybe if you'd remembered that, you wouldn't have set me up."

"Molly, put the gun down," Jack said calmly. "Did you call the police?"

"No time. Everything happened so fast here I haven't had a chance." She peered at Sol's bleeding arm and feigned shock. "Oh, that looks bad. I may have hit an artery. You could use an ambulance, Chief."

There was no mistaking the mocking tone in her voice. Jack knew he was losing control of the situation. Molly was supposed to have called the police and nothing else. She was entirely off script and didn't seem to care that Sol could die.

"Molly, please give me the gun."

She stepped away from the men, the gun still pointed at Sol Gardener. "Can't do that, Jack. This is between the Chief and me. You're just an innocent retiree who got in the middle of this. I'm the one who's lost everything. The best thing you could do is jump in your rental and drive away."

"Uh-huh, Nelson."

Sol groaned in pain. "Nelson, if you're gonna take me out then just do it."

Molly wiped a tear from her cheek. "That's exactly what I should do. What have I got left? You took it all from me, Chief."

"It was business. Just business. I think you're a straight-up cop. One of the best detectives I've ever seen. I'm sorry this happened to you."

Before Jack could process the meaning of his last words, Sol pulled Jack's gun from behind his back and fired at Molly. Three slugs hit Sol in the chest, but he managed to discharge a single round into her left thigh. She went down, and Jack rushed to her.

"Shit!" Molly hissed. "It's not a big deal. Go check on him." She motioned toward Sol, the unmistakable gurgling sounds of death coming from his throat.

Sirens echoed in the distance, but Jack doubted any paramedic could save Sol. He leaned over him, his eyes cloudy. He'd deliberately drawn on Molly, knowing that she would instinctively fire. It was better to die than face prison. He grabbed Jack's arm and pulled him closer.

"Ari. Help Ari," he whispered.

"Ari's fine, Sol. Don't worry about her."

"No, she's not. There's someone… She'll need you…"

His lifeless body sunk back against the concrete. Jack bit his lip. Sol Gardener spent his last breath for his godchild Ari—not his wife, not his own children. It was a warning. *He's concerned for Ari. Why?*

The flashing lights of an ambulance pierced the black night and the wailing sirens were deafening. Molly remained stoic against the pain as the emergency crews attended to her. Jack brought the first on-the-scene patrol officers up to speed before he returned to Molly who had several EMT's swarming around her.

"Thanks for your help, Nelson. You doin' okay?"

"Great," she said through clenched teeth. "What did Sol say there at the end?"

"The usual. He was sorry for what he'd done, and he wanted me to apologize to his wife and kids for everything."

Molly shook her head, oblivious to his lie. "I still can't believe it."

They moved her onto a stretcher and wheeled her to an ambulance. Jack noticed two local news trucks pulling up to the garage. This was going to be big news. He and Molly would inevitably spend days talking to Internal Affairs and the county prosecutors. He imagined that some local talking head looking for a job at a national network would eventually dig deep enough to learn about Molly's DUI and her subsequent resignation. And probably her alcoholism, too.

As the ambulance drove away, he shook his head. Her entire life was about to be exposed and he doubted she would ever be the same.

"Um, excuse me, are you Big Jack Adams?"

He turned to face a cherubic young face with bright eyes.

"Yup, that's me," he answered.

The rookie glanced at his partner, who shuffled his feet and appeared to be equally green. "Uh, well, the plainclothes guys aren't here yet and we're not sure what to do."

Jack cracked a grin. "What's your name, son?"

"McCoy, sir. Sean McCoy."

"Well, McCoy, first, we need to secure the crime scene. Why don't you boys go get your notebooks?"

They scurried off to the patrol car while Jack took a deep breath. Sol's last words. *She'll need you.*

He shook his head. "So much for retirement."

**Publications from
Bella Books, Inc.**
Women. Books. Even Better Together.
**P.O. Box 10543
Tallahassee, FL 32302
Phone: 800-729-4992
www.bellabooks.com**

CALM BEFORE THE STORM by Peggy J. Herring. Colonel Marcel Robideaux doesn't tell and so far no one official has asked, but the amorous pursuit by Jordan McGowan has her worried for both her career and her honor.
978-0-9677753-1-9

THE WILD ONE by Lyn Denison. Rachel Weston is busy keeping home and head together after the death of her husband. Her kids need her and what she doesn't need is the confusion that Quinn Farrelly creates in her body and heart.
978-0-9677753-4-0

LESSONS IN MURDER by Claire McNab. There's a corpse in the school with a neat hole in the head and a Black & Decker drill alongside. Which teacher should Inspector Carol Ashton suspect? Unfortunately, the alluring Sybil Quade is at the top of the list. First in this highly lauded series.
978-1-931513-65-4

WHEN AN ECHO RETURNS by Linda Kay Silva. The bayou where Echo Branson found her sanity has been swept clean by a hurricane — or at least they thought. Then an evil washed up by the storm comes looking for them all, one-by-one. Second in series.
978-1-59493-225-0

DEADLY INTERSECTIONS by Ann Roberts. Everyone is lying, including her own father and her girlfriend. Leaving matters to the professionals is supposed to be easier! Third in series with *PAID IN FULL* and *WHITE OFFERINGS*.
978-1-59493-224-3

SUBSTITUTE FOR LOVE by Karin Kallmaker. No substitutes, ever again! But then Holly's heart, body and soul are captured by Reyna... Reyna with no last name and a secret life that hides a terrible bargain, one written in family blood.
978-1-931513-62-3

MAKING UP FOR LOST TIME by Karin Kallmaker. Take one Next Home Network Star and add one Little White Lie to equal mayhem in little Mendocino and a recipe for sizzling romance. This lighthearted, steamy story is a feast for the senses in a kitchen that is way too hot.
978-1-931513-61-6

2ND FIDDLE by Kate Calloway. Cassidy James's first case left her with a broken heart. At least this new case is fighting the good fight, and she can throw all her passion and energy into it.
978-1-59493-200-7

HUNTING THE WITCH by Ellen Hart. The woman she loves — used to love — offers her help, and Jane Lawless finds it hard to say no. She needs TLC for recent injuries and who better than a doctor? But Julia's jittery demeanor awakens Jane's curiosity. And Jane has never been able to resist a mystery. #9 in series and Lammy-winner.
978-1-59493-206-9

FAÇADES by Alex Marcoux. Everything Anastasia ever wanted — she has it. Sidney is the woman who helped her get it. But keeping it will require a price — the unnamed passion that simmers between them.
978-1-59493-239-7

ELENA UNDONE by Nicole Conn. The risks. The passion. The devastating choices. The ultimate rewards. Nicole Conn rocked the lesbian cinema world with Claire of the Moon and has rocked it again with Elena Undone. This is the book that tells it all…
978-1-59493-254-0

WHISPERS IN THE WIND by Frankie J. Jones. It began as a camping trip, then a simple hike. Dixon Hayes and Elizabeth Colter uncover an intriguing cave on their hike, changing their world, perhaps irrevocably.
978-1-59493-037-9

WEDDING BELL BLUES by Julia Watts. She'll do anything to save what's left of her family. Anything. It didn't seem like a bad plan...at first. Hailed by readers as Lammy-winner Julia Watts' funniest novel.
978-1-59493-199-4

WILDFIRE by Lynn James. From the moment botanist Devon McKinney meets ranger Elaine Thomas the chemistry is undeniable. Sharing — and protecting — a mountain for the length of their short assignments leads to unexpected passion in this sizzling romance by newcomer Lynn James.
978-1-59493-191-8

LEAVING L.A. by Kate Christie. Eleanor Chapin is on the way to the rest of her life when Tessa Flanaghan offers her a lucrative summer job caring for Tessa's daughter Laya. It's only temporary and everyone expects Eleanor to be leaving L.A...
978-1-59493-221-2

SOMETHING TO BELIEVE by Robbi McCoy. When Lauren and Cassie meet on a once-in-a-lifetime river journey through China their feelings are innocent…at first. Ten years later, nothing — and everything — has changed. From Golden Crown winner Robbi McCoy.
978-1-59493-214-4

DEVIL'S ROCK: THE SEARCH FOR PATRICK DOE by Gerri Hill. Deputy Andrea Sullivan and Agent Cameron Ross vow to bring a killer to justice. The killer has other plans. Gerri Hill pens another intriguing blend of mystery and romance in this page-turning thriller.
978-1-59493-218-2

SHADOW POINT by Amy Briant. Madison Maguire has just been not-quite fired, told her brother is dead and discovered she has to pick up a five-year old niece she's never met. After she makes it to Shadow Point it seems like someone—or something—doesn't want her to leave. Romance sizzles in this ghost story from Amy Briant.
978-1-59493-216-8

JUKEBOX by Gina Daggett. Debutantes in love. With each other. Two young women chafe at the constraints of parents and society with a friendship that could be more, if they can break free. Gina Daggett is best known as "Lipstick" of the columnist duo Lipstick & Dipstick.
978-1-59493-212-0

BLIND BET by Tracey Richardson. The stakes are high when Ellen Turcotte and Courtney Langford meet at the blackjack tables. Lady Luck has been smiling on Courtney but Ellen is a wild card she may not be able to handle.
978-1-59493-211-3